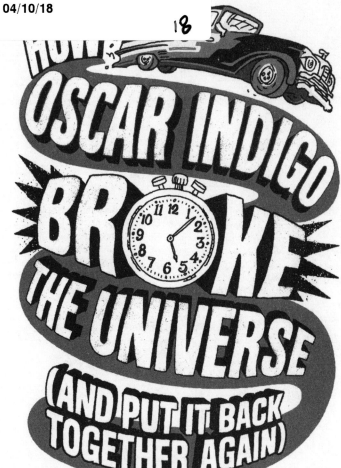

DAVID TEAGUE

HARPER
An Imprint of HarperCollinsPublishers

ISBN 978-0-06-237749-4

Typography by Ellice M. Lee
17 18 19 20 21   CG/LSCH   10 9 8 7 6 5 4 3 2
❖
First Edition

For Phil Stamps, Miss Temple,
Ethel Beatrice Warfield Teague, and everybody
who ever hit a walk-off backyard homer

What is there to say about a guy with a batting average of .000 and nothing to show for four years on the team but a total of six errors and a shelf full of participation trophies?

Hold on to your box seat. You're about to find out.

Oscar Indigo's smile blazed as perpetually as the twin suns of Kepler-47, his enthusiasm could've powered a midsize Philadelphia suburb, and his determination matched that of the universally admired honeybee. Oscar refused to consider failure an option, even when it cast a longer shadow across his life than Yankee Stadium casts across the Bronx.

Oscar never quit.

Even when the fate of the universe hung in the balance. . . .

OscarAde

On a warm evening in early July, Oscar and his teammates—Dusty Hanrahan, Bobby Farouk, Carl "Carlissimo" Fong, Axel Machado, Steve Brinkley, Kevin Truax, Kamran Singh, Layton Brooks, and Lourdes Mangubat—gathered around their coach, Ron Hansen.

It was the bottom of the ninth in the first game of their three-game championship series against the West Mt. Etna Yankees. This game was the biggest contest in the history of Oscar's Slugger League team, the East Mt. Etna Wildcats, perennial punch line of Marlborough County, Pennsylvania. The summer sun had set. Bats chased moths through the glittering white beams of the stadium lights, and the aroma of popcorn wafted across the Mt. Etna diamond.

Coach Ron said, "Wildcats, I know our season didn't turn out like we expected. None of us is prepared for the situation we now face." The coach gazed in wide-eyed bafflement at his black baseball shoes. "I don't know what happened. I don't know what to say." He shook his head at the enormous riddle he found himself contemplating. "But we're only behind by one run, and if we score just twice, we'll defeat the West Mt. Etna Select Elite Pro-Development Yankees to take the lead in the Slugger League Championship Series!" He smiled distractedly at his team and said, "Which has never happened before in the history of the Wildcats?" Over the years, Coach Ron had gotten so used to losing, he couldn't quite wrap his mind around the thought that now the Wildcats might win.

The team members stared at one another, shuffled their feet, and wondered if their coach was ever going to learn how to give a decent pep talk.

Then Coach Ron's glance fell upon Oscar, who was sitting on the bench, where he'd sat all game, every game, since April. Due to the aforementioned microscopic batting average and high error count.

Oscar couldn't help it. A spark of hope blazed in his

chest. Was the coach going to put him in, even though he hadn't played for months? Maybe, Oscar thought, Coach Ron could finally see that down deep inside him there was an unstoppable combination of positive attitude and undiscovered talent that would make him the perfect guy to win the game, despite all evidence to the contrary. Silently, Oscar pleaded, *Put me in, Coach.*

"Oscar!" said Coach Ron.

"Yes?" said Oscar.

"Tell us one of your inspirational stories!" ordered the coach.

"Sure, Coach," sighed Oscar. His hopes of playing blew away in the summer breeze like so much infield dust, and his spirits wavered. But he recovered quickly and launched into one of the many rousing baseball tales he knew by heart.

"In game six of the 1975 World Series," began Oscar, "Carlton Fisk of the Boston Red Sox came to bat in the bottom of the twelfth. The game was tied. Carlton swatted a pitch high down the left-field line. It looked like a home run! A win for the Sox! But no! As the ball dropped, it drifted foul. Boston saw its chance slipping away. That's when Carlton started jumping up and down. That's when Carlton started waving at the ball to stay in play. Hope radiated from inside Carlton. And the ball swerved one eighth of an inch right and bounced off the foul pole into fair territory! A home run! Boston Red Sox 7, Cincinnati Reds 6."

"Perfect. Thanks, Oscar," said the Coach. "Now. Who's up? Bobby Farouk? Bobby, march yourself out there and go all *Carlton Fisk* on the West Mt. Etna Yankees!"

Bobby made his way to the plate. Truthfully, Bobby was a little uncoordinated. When Bobby swung at the ball, he looked like he was trying to swat a particularly pesky horsefly with his bat, but his unorthodox style tended to distract pitchers, and he got a surprising number of hits.

Unfortunately, today's pitcher happened to be Taser Tompkins, four-time Slugger League All-Star, who wasn't fazed by anything. Taser let his first pitch fly, and Bobby swung his bat, but he only managed to graze the top of Taser's curve ball, dribbling a slow roller in front of the plate, which the catcher, Bifferato "Bif" Stroganoff, scooped up and threw to first before Bobby could take three steps.

"Way to go, Bobby!" cried Oscar. "You almost got a hit!"

"Thanks, Oscar," said Bobby on the way back to the dugout, even though he hadn't really come close.

Steve Brinkley clattered across the dugout. Steve

actually had a very special talent, which Oscar had spotted after a hundred innings of watching him from the bench. Steve was spectacularly nearsighted. He could barely see past the end of his own eyelashes. So when he batted, he stood so close to the plate, squinting at pitches, that he was nearly inside the strike zone. Which meant he was a magnet for beanballs.

"Just don't swing at anything, Steve," Oscar whispered as Steve passed by, "and try to get yourself hit by a pitch."

And for good luck, he handed Steve a cup of Oscar-Ade.

OscarAde, you ask? This unusual drink was one of Oscar's biggest contributions to the Wildcats, the symbol of his overwhelming love for baseball. OscarAde was a secret recipe that called for a half pound of Gatorade powder, six gallons of water from the infield irrigation hose, and one drop of Oscar's dad's Old Spice aftershave. The final ingredient may explain why Oscar kept the recipe secret.

Some people thought drinking it brought good fortune. Other people had trouble choking it down. And many people held both of these opinions about OscarAde at the same time. For instance, Steve.

So Steve knocked back the OscarAde in one gulp

while holding his nose. "Thanks, Oscar," he gasped.

"You're welcome, Steve," said Oscar.

At bat, Steve took Oscar's advice and stood close to the plate, and on the first pitch, he took a fastball to the elbow.

"Take your base!" cried the ump.

Steve did.

"Way to go!" called Oscar, pumping his fist in triumph.

Steve pumped his fist right back. Maybe to see if his arm still worked after the 77-mile-per-hour pitch caromed off his funny bone before grazing his ankle and skittering under the backstop. Or maybe to say thanks for the advice. Whatever it was, while Steve was busy gesticulating at Oscar, he absentmindedly took his foot off the bag. Taser fired the ball to the first baseman and picked him off.

Two outs. Not looking good for the Wildcats.

Kamran Singh, the left fielder, four and a half feet high and weighing as much as a heavy breakfast, leaped up and said in outrage, "What kind of universe is this, anyway? We did everything right! We did everything we're supposed to! We came to warm-ups early and did our stretches, and I took all my library books back on time! And the West Mt. Etna Yankees are jerks! Taser

Tompkins's mom parked her Range Rover in the handi-capped space. Robocop Roberts's mom booed us *during batting practice*. And now they're gonna win?"

"It's OK, Kamran!" said Oscar. "We've got this. I know it. Everything will work out fine."

And then, as if to prove Oscar's point, Axel Machado managed to swat a single to left. One runner on base.

The Wildcats all cheered, and over their delighted voices, the coach called, "Mangubat! You're up!"

The team sighed in relief. For if anybody was going to win this game, it was the Wildcats' newest player, Lourdes Mangubat, who'd arrived from Texas at the beginning of the season. Just aspiring to be half as good as Lourdes had made the rest of the Wildcats three times better. You can do the math, but however you calculate it, they owed their season's success to her. When Lourdes batted, opposing pitchers shook in their spikes. She looked like a statue in the Philadelphia Museum of Art: Artemis, Greek goddess of the hunt, stalking mythical creatures who didn't stand a chance. Even a three-time all-star like Taser Tompkins barely had a prayer against her.

Lourdes rarely talked to the other Wildcats, except to holler "mine" when a pop fly came her way or to par-ticipate in the team cheer, which, by the way, Oscar had made up: *East Mt. Etna, East Mt. Etna, East Mt. Etna, Wow! Ain't nobody gonna keep the Wildcats down!* Try as he might, he'd never quite come up with a perfect rhyme to end it.

Some folks said Lourdes rarely spoke because she'd been born in the Philippines and her English wasn't great.

Others said maybe she felt like she was too good to talk to regular people.

Oscar thought she was probably just busy thinking about baseball.

He silently handed Lourdes her helmet, her bat, and a cup of OscarAde for good luck.

In coming years, when he looked back on this moment, he could never be sure what happened next.

Somehow, the OscarAde slipped. It plummeted to the steps and splattered all over. Lourdes's spikes slid across the slick cement. Her elbow clonked Oscar on the head. But that didn't matter. His head was hard. What mattered was Lourdes's foot, specifically, her pinky toe, which she'd jammed against one of the dugout pillars.

Lourdes crumpled to the floor in pain.

"I'm sorry! I'm sorry!" cried Oscar.

Lourdes managed to pull herself to a sitting position. And she actually said something: "Ouch."

"Ice, Oscar, ice!" cried the coach as he ripped Lourdes's shoe off.

Now, after all the years he'd spent in the dugout fetching things for people who actually played, Oscar also happened to be an ace at ice. He calmly scooped a handful out of the cooler, wrapped it in a compression bandage, and gave it to Coach Ron to apply to Lourdes's toe. But despite their valiant efforts at first aid, the toe was already the size of a Chilean grape.

"I can't believe I did this!" cried Oscar as the toe continued ballooning, now approaching California plum size. "We were about to win!"

"The score is 0–1," Bobby Farouk reminded him.

"But Lourdes was coming to bat, and she always smacks a homer when the game is on the line, and Axel is on first, so things were fine until I spilled the—"

Mr. Farouk, the umpire, who was also Bobby's granddad, stuck his head into the dugout. "You planning to send a batter out here, Coach?" he demanded.

"Right. Sure, Mr. Umpire," said Coach Ron. "Just give us one second."

"I'll give you exactly *fifteen* seconds," harrumphed the ump. "And then you forfeit."

"Lourdes?" said Coach Ron hopefully.

Lourdes tried to stand. She turned green, tears appeared at the corners of her eyes, a squeak escaped from somewhere deep inside her, and she sat back down, shaking her head.

Oscar saw Coach Ron gaze up the dugout, and he saw Coach Ron gaze down the dugout. He saw the coach check his lineup card. He saw the coach's eyes fall on him. Oscar, who was busy icing the lump on his head where Lourdes's elbow had whacked him, quickly hid the ice pack behind his back.

The coach checked his roster one more time.

Unfortunately for the Wildcats, the date was July 5.

Three Wildcats were still not back from celebrating the Fourth of July at the Jersey Shore.

Oscar Indigo was the only substitute on Coach Ron's list.

And the rules of Slugger League baseball plainly stated that if the coach wanted to keep his team eligible, he'd have to use Oscar to fill Lourdes Mangubat's spot.

"Grab a bat, Oscar." Coach Ron sighed. "You're going in."

Both hope and fear flared inside Oscar. He was going into the game. Maybe *he'd* smack a homer. Maybe he'd win the whole thing! Or, on the other hand, if history was any guide, he'd probably just—

"Try your best," advised the coach glumly. "That's all anybody can ask." He did his darnedest to sound encouraging, but he couldn't hide the gloom in his voice, and the faces of Oscar's teammates reflected similar emotions. No doubt they were remembering all the times over the years when Oscar had walked to the plate with enthusiasm, hope, and a bat nearly as tall as himself, and struck out.

On the mound, Taser emitted a scornful chortle. He set his feet. He peered down at his catcher, Bif Stroganoff, and then as he returned his attention to Oscar, a mocking grin spread across his face. He wound up and let go a blazing fastball.

Oscar swung. He missed by ten feet.

"Steeerike one!" cried the ump.

"Not good," Oscar murmured to himself. He called time to collect his thoughts. An optimistic smile played across his face, a little higher on the left than on the right, as he visualized swatting a home run.

Unfortunately, it *really* made Taser mad when losers like Oscar stood at the plate smiling hopeful smiles, acting like somewhere, in their wildest dreams, they imagined they might in a million years get a hit off him. He despised dinky, thin people who thought they mattered in the world, because they didn't. Cold ferocity beamed from Taser's eyes.

"Uh-oh," said Bif from behind Oscar. "Watch out, little dude. He's mad."

Taser came set on the mound. The world waited the way the world always waits when a pitcher goes into his motion.

Taser delivered.

With the speed of a comet, the pitch sizzled through the air. Right toward the middle of the plate. The outfield lights seemed to flare, dazzling Oscar's eyes. His high hopes abandoned him, and he was left with nothing but a shaky feeling under his ribs. The crowd noise became a pulsating hiss, and the eyes of the opposing players gleamed accusingly, as if they all knew he knew he didn't belong in the batter's box, clutching a bat, with the season's most important game on the line.

The ball seemed to travel so fast, it started scrambling light particles and gravity waves as it came, so by the time it arrived, Oscar could hardly see it. But his brain was screaming—*You have to get a hit! You have to get a hit!* Desperately, he swiped at the ball. He spun three times and fell.

As he collided with the ground, he heard:

"Steeeeee-rike two!"

"Oscar," cried Coach Ron, "calm down, fella!"

In his head, Oscar began to hear the voices of Vern Handler and Suzy Armando of CSPN—his favorite announcers—commenting on the game as if it were nationally televised. He often whiled away time in the dugout dreaming up things they might say about the Wildcats, and now they appeared in his imagination to narrate his on-field exploits:

Oscar Indigo seems a bit overwhelmed by the competition, Suzy.

That's a polite way to put it, Vern.

Oscar climbed to his feet and squinted at the stands to make sure Vern and Suzy weren't really there with their microphones, speaking into the cameras. Nope. Just the moms and dads of Mt. Etna. Vern and Suzy were only in his brain.

Oscar tapped his bat against his beat-up shoes like the pros do on TV, and he stepped into the batter's box to swing again.

As he turned to face Taser, he reached into his uniform pocket for a fraction of a second, brushing a hidden, smooth, rounded object with his fingertips. *No*, he quickly told himself, *better not*. Hastily, he pulled his hand out and settled in to bat.

Oscar noticed Lourdes Mangubat watching from the dugout as she balanced on her good foot. He was surprised by her expression. She looked like she thought he had a chance.

Suzy and Vern didn't sound so sure.

I wonder if Oscar does indeed have a chance, Vern.

I'd like to think so, Suzy. He seems like a nice kid. But—

Taser's next pitch came scorching through the night. Some kind of curveball, traveling so fast it seemed to bend cosmic laws nobody had discovered yet, dropping from shoulder level to knee height in the blink of an eye. The ball appeared to vanish as it flew past, but there was no mistaking the smack it made in Bif Stroganoff's mitt, or the sound of Mr. Farouk, the umpire, calling.

"Ball one," declared the ump.

Taser had missed the strike zone. *Yes!* thought Oscar. He wasn't dead yet.

"Sit that little wimp down so we can go get ice cream!" screeched a voice from the seats behind Oscar.

Taser shot the kind of glance into the stands that you shoot your mother when you've got things under control and don't need her input. He toed the rubber for his fourth pitch. He and Bif exchanged signals.

I don't envy young Indigo, Vern.

Me, either, Suzy.

Oscar called time. He backed out of the batter's box. He reached into his uniform pocket to touch the smooth object again. And despite his reservations about what he was about to do, Oscar slid the object out carefully, very carefully, so no one could see: an antique watch. It looked like the ones railroad conductors in his mom's old black-and-white movies sometimes pulled from their vests to scrutinize through narrowed eyes before bellowing, "All aboard for New York City," whereupon the train began transporting the hero toward his destiny. But Oscar knew its true purpose.

Stepping back into the box, he palmed the watch between his left hand and the bat.

Taser hurled the baseball. It shot toward Oscar like a ballistic missile.

Delicately, so no one could see, Oscar pushed the red button atop the watch hidden in his palm, and Taser Tompkins's fastball halted dead in the air right in front of him. And along with the ball, the Yankees fielders, the Wildcats in the dugout, and the fans in the bleachers suddenly froze. Birds stopped in the sky, jets halted on their flight paths. Planets hovered in their orbits, and all around

Oscar, the fundamental processes of the universe ceased. In the stillness, Oscar drew back his bat and clobbered the eerily dangling baseball with all his might, sending it soaring over Taser Tompkins's big fat head.

Earlier That Morning

This might be the time to discuss where that watch came from.

Let's back up approximately twelve hours, to 9:03 am. Oscar stood in front of his house blinking in the yellow sunlight and green shade of his neighborhood, which was called Brook Meadow, even though it had no brook and had no meadow. Jennifer Street, which was his street, quit at the edge of Tuscarora Woods, forming a cul-de-sac in which it was safe to play baseball because cars never drove around it.

Oscar balanced a baseball on his batting tee. Overhead, the sun burned the color of a lemon. The sky looked blue enough to drink. The leaves of Tuscarora Woods rustled in the morning breeze. A jay winged overhead screaming "Thief! Thief!" for reasons best known to itself.

Oscar cocked his bat, narrowed his eyes, imagined he was hitting for the Phillies in the World Series, and swung for all he was worth.

Whiffffffff. Oscar opened his eyes. The ball was still perched on the tee like a sparrow atop a maple tree.

Just then, Steve Brinkley—that's right, the nearsighted guy who is going to get himself dinged on the elbow in the game a little later—rolled up on his skateboard, glasses glinting in the morning sun. He said, "How'd you miss that?"

"I don't know," replied Oscar ruefully.

"Even *I* can hit a ball off a tee," said Steve. "Give me the bat."

Steve took the bat, squared up, and swatted the ball. It rose into the morning air, then dropped with a thud against the front door of Oscar's neighbor: Eleanor Ethel Ellington, age eighty-five.

Oscar and Steve both held their breaths. But no sign of Miss Ellington. Phew. Miss Ellington was just about the nicest eighty-five-year-old lady you could ever hope to meet, but she still objected to baseballs banging off her house.

Oscar fetched the ball and put it back on the tee.

"How about if you pretend you're somebody else?" asked Steve. "Somebody who can really hit."

"Like who?" asked Oscar.

"Hank Aaron?" said Steve.

"OK. I'm Hank Aaron," said Oscar. He swung. He missed.

"Maybe you need a more modern example," said Steve. "Try Big Papi. David Ortiz."

Oscar imagined he was Big Papi. He whiffed.

"Wow. OK," said Steve. "Try Dottie Kamenshek."

"Who?" said Oscar.

"Dottie Kamenshek of the All-American Girls Professional Baseball League," clarified Steve. "Seven-time all-star. She had one of the highest batting averages in history. Some people even wanted her to play in the men's leagues. There's a movie based on her."

"OK," said Oscar. "Fine, Steve. I'll be Dottie Kamenshek. Why not?"

This time, the air turbulence from his passing bat blew the ball off the tee. It bounced on the pavement.

"That's a little better!" said Steve. "How about Babe Ruth?"

"Ummmmm . . . ," Oscar said. "I don't know, this

doesn't seem to be working."

"But the Bambino was the greatest hitter of all time!" exclaimed Steve.

"I know who Babe Ruth is!" said Oscar. "It's just—he could be a jerk sometimes."

"We're pretending, Oscar," Steve pointed out. "I think it'll be OK for you to be Babe Ruth, even if he was mean once in a while."

Dr. Soul, Oscar's orange cat, made his way across the grass and took a seat on the curb to watch.

"I'm just going to be Oscar," said Oscar. He eyed the ball. He swung. He made contact. The ball flew eleven feet. Well. It was better than nothing. "Yes!" cried Oscar. "The crowd goes wild! *Oscar! Oscar! Oscar Indigo!*"

His daydream faded. The shouting didn't.

"Oscar! Oscar! Oscar Indigo!"

Oscar blinked himself back to reality in time to see Steve fleeing down the street on his board faster than the neighborhood speed limit and Dr. Soul hightailing it for the woods.

"Goodness gracious, Oscar!" the voice continued. "Pay attention! Be aware of your surroundings! What kind of boy stands around dreaming in the middle of the road?

What if the recycling truck comes by?"

Oscar turned and saw, standing with her hands on her hips, gray hair flying in the morning breeze, his neighbor, Miss Eleanor Ethel Ellington.

Eleanor Ethel Ellington

"Try keeping your eyes on the ball when you swing," suggested Miss Ellington. She had a habit of sneaking up on him and giving him batting tips. Usually, this happened when he was standing around day-dreaming about imaginary game-time exploits and forgot to keep an eye out for her.

"I do," said Oscar.

"Hmmm," said Miss Ellington. "If you say so. Oscar, I would like to request your assistance." She beckoned him from the knee-deep tangle of vines that passed for her lawn.

"Sure, Miss Ellington," sighed Oscar, because in his next-door-neighbor's dictionary, *request* meant the same thing as *demand*. And he could never turn her down.

Oscar followed her through rampant vegetation to the

garden in the middle of her backyard. It featured rows of beans and peas and tomato plants growing in wire cages. Miss Ellington put her hands on her hips to catch her breath. "We need to water," she finally said.

Oscar knew the drill from experience. He and Miss Ellington had been pals a long time. He lifted a rusty watering can from its hook on the side of her garden shed and held it under the spigot of the cistern that caught rain flowing from the downspout leading from the roof. Crystal-clear water splashed against the bottom.

"Hurry up," grouched Miss Ellington. "Do you want my tomato plants to wilt?"

Oscar would have rolled his eyes at her impatience, but the thing was, he *didn't* want the tomatoes to wilt. He liked those plants. They smelled peppery and tart when he brushed against them, and even if the tiny white prickles on the undersides of the leaves made his skin itch, he still wanted the bushes to grow tall and healthy in the small, black, bowl-shaped hollows of dirt he and Miss Ellington had planted them in the last time she'd "requested" his help. He *wanted* them to bear ruby-red tomatoes, and he wanted to help pick those tomatoes and load them into the basket of Miss Ellington's giant adult tricycle so she could take them down to the farmer's market to sell them.

And he wanted to take the two tomatoes she always gave him for helping at harvest, and slice them and make them into bacon, lettuce, and tomato sandwiches to share with his mom.

And even though it was hard to admit, he really kind of hoped that next year, Miss Ellington would find him standing in front of his house and "request" his help to start the process all over.

Just thinking about it made him feel like part of something bigger than himself.

"Are you going to water the tomatoes or stand there staring into space all morning?" asked Miss Ellington.

"I'm going to water," replied Oscar. Miss Ellington could get a little bossy. Oscar didn't mind. She was his friend.

As he moved from plant to plant, Miss Ellington watched like a hawk over his shoulder, making sure he didn't pour too little or too much. This was a bit nerve-wracking, but Oscar had gotten used to Miss Ellington's habits. At the last tomato plant, which was twice as high as the rest, and stronger and greener and seemed to have an almost infinite number of branches rippling and swaying in the wind, Miss Ellington paused, reached among the leaves, sank her fingernails into the base of a small, withered branch, ruthlessly pinched it off, and tossed it over the garden fence into Tuscarora Woods. "That one wasn't going to grow any tomatoes," she remarked when she saw his face. She smacked her palms together. "We're better off without it."

Oscar nodded and shook the last few drops out of the can. Miss Ellington said, "Finished? You must be thirsty after all this work."

"I'll just have a glass of water at home," replied Oscar. "But thank you."

"Come inside and enjoy my hospitality!" ordered Miss Ellington.

Mothballs

"Is there something wrong with your drink?" asked Miss Ellington as Oscar stared into his hot chocolate on her kitchen table.

"No," said Oscar. "It's fine."

And yes, if you left out the fact that Miss Ellington had made it from a six-year-old can of discount instant hot chocolate powder mixed up in warm water from the faucet, Oscar wouldn't even have been lying. Theoretically, the hot chocolate should have been just fine.

The marshmallows were the problem.

They lurked in the shadows of Miss Ellington's pantry, month after month, year after year, dehydrated to a hardness exceeding that of mastodon bones by the air of Miss Ellington's house, which reeked of mothballs and made everything else in her house reek of mothballs, too. Gaaaah.

"Way back in the Dark Ages, when I was a girl," declared Miss Ellington, "my friends and I always said the best thing on a hot day is a hot drink!" Oscar nodded. Over the years, he'd heard a lot of bizarre things Miss Ellington and her friends used to say to each other.

He glanced at the thermometer screwed to the back porch railing, which read ninety-two.

He brought his mothball-flavored hot chocolate to his lips.

"You've got a big game tonight," Miss Ellington observed.

Oscar lowered the mug. "Against the Yankees. The first game of the Slugger League Championship Series."

"When you go to up to bat, keep your eyes on the ball," said Miss Ellington.

"You told me that outside," Oscar reminded her.

"I'm telling you again," said Miss Ellington.

"The coach won't put me in," sighed Oscar. "I mean, I appreciate the vote of confidence, but I'm not going up to bat."

"The coach *might* put you in. You *might* get to bat," insisted Miss Ellington. "You never know."

"I guess you're right," said Oscar. "I don't *know*. But I'm pretty *sure* I won't get to bat."

"You're a good kid, Oscar," said Miss Ellington. "You'll make your mark on the universe one way or the other."

"Thanks, Miss Ellington," said Oscar.

"I've got some cookies in my cupboard," continued Miss Ellington, pushing aside a crab hammer and a bottle of Lysol as she searched. "Somewhere."

"Yummy!" said Oscar, wincing at the thought of their inevitable mothball flavor.

At that moment, a powerful engine rumbled along the street outside. It shook Miss Ellington's windows. She stopped searching and glanced around uneasily.

Oscar looked around, too. He noticed for the first time that something was different about Miss Ellington's house that morning. A garden trowel lay on the kitchen sink. Muddy boots leaned in the corner. Leaves littered the floor. Mail lay scattered across one end of the kitchen table, as if she'd begun reading it but never finished.

And that was the strangest part. Miss Ellington had a very precise system for mail. She wrote letters to her friends every week, using the stationery, pens, stamps, and wax seal in the rolltop desk in her office. She put the letters in the basket of her giant tricycle—the same one she used for tomatoes—pedaled them to the post office, mailed them, and checked her box for replies.

And once in a while, when Miss Ellington felt too tired to make the trip, Oscar made it for her (although he rode his own bicycle). He liked starting Miss Ellington's letters on their journeys, picking up stamps at the post office for future letters, and bringing back answers from her friends. He liked reading the names and addresses on the envelopes and imagining the people and places. *Norman Pliner, Northfield, Minnesota. Huggsy Strathmore, Little Rock, Arkansas. Dinky Hanrahan, Los Angeles, California.* And once in a while, over stale cupcakes or a slice of pie that tasted faintly of cleaning supplies, Miss Ellington told him things about her friends. For instance, Sheila Flaherty of Seattle, Washington, had a great-grandson the same age as Oscar who was a Little League all-star shortstop.

Lately, though, Oscar realized Miss Ellington didn't mail as many letters as she had when he was younger.

Oscar glimpsed something glinting among the envelopes.

"What's this?" he asked, reaching across the table to retrieve a giant gold pocket watch. Its face glowed a faint green in the dim kitchen.

"Heavens to Betsy! Put that down!" cried Miss Ellington. She rushed over faster than Oscar had ever seen her move—and he'd seen her move plenty fast, especially when raccoons threatened her tomatoes. She snatched the watch from his hands.

"Sorry, Miss Ellington," said Oscar. "It was just— glowing a little—"

"I was contemplating the vicissitudes of time," murmured Miss Ellington, burying the watch in her pocket and gazing thoughtfully at a slit-open envelope on the table.

"OK, sure, right," said Oscar. "The vicissitudes of time. That makes sense. I guess a lot of people contemplate the vicissitudes of time. I might even do it myself once in a while. By the way, what's a vicissitude?"

"An unforeseen change," said Miss Ellington, pulling the watch from her pocket. She seemed to forget about Oscar as she studied the old watch, and in the expanding silence, he blew on his hot chocolate, kicking up a cloud of mothball-scented steam. He sneezed.

"Are you all right, Miss Ellington?" asked Oscar.

"I will be, Oscar," said Miss Ellington quietly. "Thank you for asking."

Outside, the sound of the heavy engine returned. It idled for a moment in front of Miss Ellington's house and rumbled into silence. Then a car door slammed. Heavy footfalls thudded up Miss Ellington's walk. A knock thundered against her door. Miss Ellington tottered down the wooden hallway to peek through the lace curtain in the window.

"Oscar," she said, turning back quickly. "Actually, I *would* like you to have this watch." She pitched it to him. Usually, when people threw things at Oscar, his brain short-circuited and he dropped them. But the toss took him by surprise. He didn't have time to think. So he caught it.

The banging on the door continued.

"But you just told me not to touch it," Oscar pointed out.

"But now I'm telling you to take it," said Miss Ellington.

"But—" began Oscar.

"Just take the watch and vamoose," hissed Miss Ellington. "Through the back door. Consider it a token of appreciation for helping in my garden."

"I don't have to finish the hot chocolate?" asked Oscar.

"No!" whispered Miss Ellington.

"All right!" said Oscar on behalf of his taste buds. As he made his way down the back steps, he happened to peek over his shoulder, down the hallway, as Miss Ellington opened her door to reveal two men wearing black suits. One was as big as a restaurant refrigerator, the other sized like a fifth grader. A colossal black car gleamed behind them at the curb. The sight of them made him shiver, and he paused, but behind her back, Miss Ellington shooed him with her left hand, as if, whatever was about to happen, she wanted him and the watch to play no part.

The World Atomic Clock

And that's how Oscar ended up with the watch that stopped time.

For the rest of the afternoon, he couldn't stop staring at it. Distractedly, he tried to watch a Phillies game on TV but couldn't concentrate. Briefly, he dangled a string in front of Dr. Soul, who pretended not to notice. He managed to bat a few balls off his tee but lost interest. Then he attempted to take a nap. But he kept coming back to the watch.

Strangely, there didn't seem to be any way to wind this watch, although a giant red button protruded from the top. Oscar felt tempted to mash the button, but somehow, every time he put his thumb on it, he experienced a tingle of anxiety along his spine, so he took his thumb back off.

Once, Dr. Soul leaped onto Oscar's lap for a look, but

as soon as he landed, he laid his ears back, spit, and leaped back down to crouch on the kitchen floor under Oscar's chair.

The watch, despite its mysterious origins and antique facade, kept perfect time. Oscar had compared it to the web page of the World Atomic Clock on six different occasions and always found it smack on the money.

On its back appeared a pattern of fierce swirls, which, when Oscar squinted and held his eye about five inches away, turned out to be lines of poetry, snippets of song, and words of wisdom written in minuscule letters, eddying in the gold:

. . . lost time is never found . . . there's no time like the present . . . time is an asterisk . . . it was the best of times, it was the worst of times . . . a stitch in time saves nine . . . times are tough all over . . . may you live in interesting times . . .

Reading what the watch had to say about time, Oscar paradoxically lost track of time, so he was startled when his mother interrupted his ruminations by bustling in through the garage door. "Hi, honey!" she exclaimed, sending him jumping out of his skin. "I just stopped by to say good luck at your game."

"You aren't coming?" Oscar asked, not surprised, but still disappointed.

"I have to work the night shift at Café Karaoke. I'm really sorry."

"That's OK," said Oscar, turning back to the watch. His mother worked hard, especially now that his dad had left, so Oscar couldn't blame her for missing the game.

"There's still coffee!" cried his mother, eyeballing the pot on the counter. "Hallelujah! I'm so exhausted!" And as she poured the dregs into a mug, she said, "By the way, I'm tired of finding your socks all over the house. Would you please start—"

Oscar sighed. Sometimes, he wished his mother would quit yelling at him about his socks. His thumb darted to the red button. And before he could think about what he was doing, Oscar pushed.

His mother quit yelling at him about his socks. In midsentence. The coffee she was pouring hung suspended in the air halfway between the pot and the cup.

A robin swooping down from a branch outside the kitchen window stopped dead in midflight, dangling motionless, four feet off the ground.

A car turning around in the street halted dead on the asphalt.

Dr. Soul, who had been slowly waking up under the table, froze with only one eye open. The microwave clock, the oven clock, the toaster-oven clock, and the coffee-maker clock all flashed 6:00:59.

Oscar blinked in surprise. He seemed to have frozen everything around him, including time. Yet he could still move! In an instant, he saw that the red watch button had turned green. Green, as in "go." After a count of *one Mississippi*, he pressed it again. Whereupon everything started moving once more. His mom launched back into her lecture, the coffee cascaded into the cup, the car glided past, the robin snatched its worm, Dr. Soul yawned, and all the clocks marched forward.

Oscar gazed in awe at the watch.

"—putting them in the hamper when you take them off?" His mom was still talking. "What are you staring at?" she demanded.

"Nothing," murmured Oscar as he casually covered the watch with his left hand. He wondered if that time-stopped coffee was safe to drink, but it was too late, because his mother had already guzzled it. He watched her closely for a few seconds, and to his relief, she seemed fine.

"I'll pick you up after the game," said his mother, gathering her keys and kissing him on the cheek. "Maybe I'll get there in time to see the end." The door slammed behind her.

Oscar gazed at the watch on the table in front of him. He glanced at the coffeepot. "What did I just do, Dr. Soul?" he asked. But Dr. Soul didn't answer.

A few minutes later, as he put on his uniform for the game, Oscar slipped the watch into his pants pocket. He didn't know exactly why. Maybe it was unintentional. Maybe he didn't want to leave the watch at home unattended. Or maybe, in the back of his mind, he thought he might need it for something unforeseen.

And Now, We Return to the Game

Back on the baseball diamond, as you probably remember, Oscar had just smacked the ball over Taser's head. As he watched his shot fly into the night, Oscar counted how many seconds he was keeping time stopped. This felt important, somehow, because if anybody ever demanded an exact number in the future, he felt like he should have one ready, though he really hoped nobody would ever ask.

Since he'd already used up one second in his mom's kitchen, Oscar started at two.

Two Mississippi.

The ball slowly stopped rising, and dropped, but ran out of steam and stopped in midair before it hit the ground, hanging a few feet in front of second base. *Wow,* Oscar thought sadly, *even when I cheat, I can't knock it out of the infield.*

He sighed and took off running across the diamond.

Three Mississippi. Four Mississippi.

He snatched the ball from the air above second base.

Five Mississippi. Six Mississippi. Seven.

He stopped at the edge of the outfield warning track and gingerly lifted the ball into the glare of the lights. Carefully, he let go, and just as he'd hoped, it hung where he'd put it, dangling tantalizingly above the fence in the clear summer night.

Eleven Mississippi. Twelve Mississippi. Thirteen Mississippi. Fourteen . . .

Oscar Indigo ran back to home plate, picked up his bat, struck the pose of the guy he had always dreamed of being, the guy with his bat extended toward the horizon, waiting for his home run to drop over the outfield fence. Then he pressed the glowing green button, restarting the watch, activating time once again right after he got to *nineteen Mississippi.*

The spectators and Oscar's teammates and the opposing players blinked once and sat still for an instant, as if waking from a spell. Then all eyeballs in the park fixed curiously on Oscar, because the last thing anybody remembered, he'd been standing at the plate with shaky knees, clutching his bat while waiting for the fastball that was going to strike him out. His friends had been busily thinking up nice fibs to tell him, like, for instance, it wasn't important whether he won or lost, it was how he played the game.

But now everyone saw Oscar Indigo standing triumphantly in the batter's box, waving his bat at a distant baseball as it dropped into the itchy weeds behind the outfield fence. A cheer slowly rose from the East Mt. Etna side.

Looks like a walk-off home run from young Oscar Indigo, Suzy.

Quite a feat, Vern.

The crowd went wild.

Oscar Indigo had become a hero.

Or so he told himself.

We Are the Champions

Oscar didn't have a chance to worry about the implications of freezing time for a total of nineteen seconds, because the East Mt. Etna Wildcats immediately poured onto the field, dogpiling him. He felt like he was in a movie; he felt like he'd just won the Most Valuable Player trophy; he felt like somebody somewhere was about to name a marshmallow-filled candy bar after him. He felt squashed. "Let me up!" he cried.

"Holy cats," said Axel Machado, setting Oscar on his feet. "My little sister is bigger than you. And she's in fourth grade. How'd you hit that ball so far?"

Oscar could only shrug and look at the sky and say, "Conditions must've been perfect."

And despite the balmy summer breeze tickling the

43

back of his neck, Oscar felt slightly wintry inside, because he'd just cheated, possibly on a large scale—how large, he didn't know. But as millions of stars twinkled down at him icily, something seemed out of place. He couldn't be sure, but he thought he saw a hole in the bottom of the Big Dipper.

Just then, the heavy rumble of an old car sounded in the night, and he saw the black Cadillac that had been parked outside Miss Ellington's house pass like a shadow on the street.

But his teammates' cheering soon drowned out his worries. Together, they sang "We Are the Champions" at the top of their lungs.

Vern and Suzy commented from inside his imagination.

Bona fide late-inning heroics, Suzy!

You can't stop Oscar Indigo, Vern, you can only hope to contain him!

Congratulations bubbled up all around Oscar. Congratulations sounded awfully different, he reflected, when they weren't just polite lies meant to spare his feelings.

They would have sounded even better if he'd actually earned them, but he pushed that thought away.

Once the cheering of the Wildcats' moms and dads

had faded into the night and the fact had sunk in that the East Mt. Etna Wildcats had actually just defeated the almighty West Mt. Etna Yankees to take a 1–0 lead in the championship series—and more than all that, once everybody had gotten used to the idea that Oscar Indigo was responsible for this—Kamran Singh cried, "What do we do now?"

"Line up!" called Coach Ron. "Shake hands!"

The rival teams made two lines and snaked past one another, slapping high fives as tradition demanded. Everybody said what you always say, after any game, no matter what: "Good game, good game, good game."

Except for Oscar. He tugged his jersey straight as he made his way down the line to the end, where Taser stood, and when he reached the Yankees' star, he said what he'd always promised himself he'd say to his opponent, if he ever won anything. "Congratulations."

For some reason, the sound of this word caused total silence to fall over the diamond, the field, and the parking lot for a quarter mile in every direction.

"What?" said Taser.

Oscar had actually been rehearsing this moment at home for five years, playing make-believe games with the assistance of his friend Steve and a handful of imaginary baseball heroes. After hitting a fictional walk-off home run in the street in front of his house, the next thing Oscar always did was behave like a gracious winner. So he knew just what to say. "Great effort," he told Taser, extending his hand to shake.

"You making fun of me?" Taser asked, staring straight into Oscar's eyes, ignoring his hand.

Oscar slowly let it drop. "N-n-no," he stammered. "I mean—you did a good job pitching."

"You want me to punch you?" asked Taser, stepping very close, each large hand now a fist.

"Hey!" cried an extremely tan lady wearing gold sunglasses even though the sun had set an hour before. "Where's the umpire? That's unsportsmanlike conduct!"

"It's OK," Oscar told her. "He's just—"

"I'm not talking about him. I'm talking about you!" she said to Oscar. "Hey! Umpire! This kid is taunting my son, Taser! Give him a fine, or suspend him, or whatever you do!"

"No!" said Oscar. "I wasn't taunting. I just want to tell Taser he did a good job. I just wanted to tell him—"

"Tell me what?" asked Taser.

Oscar tried to think of the things people said to the Wildcats when they lost, or said to him when he bobbled a throw or whiffed in the batter's box. And he blurted out the first thought that came to mind. "It's not whether you win or lose, Taser," he said. "It's how you play the game!"

"See!" screeched Taser's mom. "He's taunting my little boy!"

Taser laughed nastily. "Sheesh," he said. "You're a loser, even when you win!"

And with that, he shoved Oscar into the dirt.

Fifteen minutes after the celebrations ended, the field lay black under the thickening clouds, the darkened stadium lights ticked as they cooled, and Oscar shivered, alone, in the parking lot, hoping his mom would show up soon.

Across the street, in the cool blue glow of the bus kiosk, sat Lourdes Mangubat.

She glanced his way. Even though he'd never really spoken to her, and he'd just made her smash her toe, Oscar waved. She raised her arm as if to wave back, but at that moment, the bus pulled up to the curb, hiding Lourdes, and when it pulled away, she was gone.

Now that was a bit of a disappointment, Suzy.

I have to agree, Vern.

Oscar also had to agree with the imaginary Vern.

He shivered as he walked down the block to wait for

his mother under a streetlamp, and he couldn't shake a growing sense of foreboding. As soon as he leaned against the lamppost, the bulb blinked out.

That wasn't a good sign.

Slowly, almost fearfully, Oscar slipped the giant gold watch out of his pocket again and regarded it nervously in the flicker of faraway lightning. Maybe, he was starting to realize, it would've been a good idea to learn a little more about how the watch worked before he'd pushed the big red button on top and halted time just so the Wildcats could beat the Yankees.

9:17:47, it read as the second hand swept around the dial. *9:17:48, 9:17:49, 9:17:50* . . .

He didn't even need to check the World Atomic Clock to know that it now ran nineteen seconds behind the rest of the world. And the solar system, and the galaxy, and the universe.

A gust of wind blasted across the deserted parking lot.

A flock of blackbirds squawked to life in the beech trees behind the stands. They screeched toward him through the sky. Illuminated by a lightning flash, this one much closer than the earlier flickers, they appeared not to be birds at all. They looked like very small, flying . . . dinosaurs?

But just as suddenly as they'd appeared, they disappeared. It was only a trick of the light, Oscar told himself.

The wind now held steady.

Thunder rolled.

Suddenly, a dazzling flash blinded him. From very near by. Half a block away. He flinched. A sound began to grow like a gorilla jamming trash cans into a wood chipper. And it soon became apparent that the glare wasn't lightning; it was headlights. Or one headlight, anyway. Approaching at high speed. Aiming straight for him. Tires screeched. A horn honked. And a small, rattly car ground to a halt at the curb. At the wheel sat Oscar's mom.

Just then, rain began to pelt Oscar in buckets and sheets. He fumbled with the obstinate door latch and scrambled into the car. His mother pulled away from the curb and made a U-turn in the opposite direction from the neat yards and lamplit streets of West Mt. Etna, crossing the invisible line into East Mt. Etna. Oscar gazed out the car window at mostly empty shopping centers containing only sad and neglected thrift shops that sold used clothes to families who would wear them awhile and then bring them back to be sold again, and he watched whole blocks of boarded-up houses slide by outside the glass, and he saw a factory surrounded by a rusty chain link fence secured by a padlocked gate.

"I'm sorry, honey. I couldn't get away from work," said his mother. "At least I got here before the storm hit. Sort of."

"Thanks, Mom," said Oscar, shivering as he glanced through the windshield at the strengthening rain. His anxiety must've shown on his face.

"Don't worry about the game," said his mother, noticing his look. "You'll do better next time. After all, you had to play the Yankees. They're the best! And it's the championship series! Nobody thought you guys would ever get this far."

Oscar could tell his mother had expected the Wildcats to lose and had prepared a list of comforting things to say.

"Mom," said Oscar, turning toward her. "We won."

"Good one!" she said, laughing. "You are a such a great kid! No matter what, your sense of humor always shines."

"I'm not joking," Oscar said. "We beat the Yankees. We're ahead in the series."

"I've had a long day, buster," his mother replied. "Don't mess with me."

"I'm not messing with you," said Oscar, grinning finally, even as the rain fell ferociously, flooding the streets here and there. "We won!"

"Really? How?" asked his mother, a hint of disbelief rising in her voice, although she smiled brightly to disguise it.

"It wasn't easy. Lourdes got hurt. And she's our star," said Oscar. "But I guess we just put it all together right at the end, when it counted!"

"So the Wildcats scored a bunch of points," said Oscar's mom.

"We call them 'runs' in baseball, Mom," said Oscar. "The final score was 2–1. It was really exciting."

"And this was all in the fourth quarter?" asked his mother.

"No, Mom—baseball has innings," said Oscar. "Not quarters." He had only been having these conversations with her since he was seven. One day, he still hoped, she'd figure out the great sport of baseball. As in, you scored runs, not points, and you played innings, not quarters. In the meantime, the overall concept still baffled her.

And he didn't quite know why, but he decided to leave out the part about Lourdes's toe, and all the Wildcats backups being at the beach, and his getting put into the game and going to the plate and smacking a "homer." And of course he didn't mention the watch he'd hidden in his palm. "We scored in the bottom of the ninth! We won right at the end," said Oscar.

"Five! Four! Three! Two! One!" cried his mom. "It's over! The crowd goes nuts! Wildcats are victorious!"

"Yeah," said Oscar. "Something like that. Except there's no clock in baseball. So the final seconds don't tick off—"

"That's it!" cried Oscar's mom, sawing her steering wheel viciously to the left and slaloming through a small lake in the middle of the road. "We're going to Rossini's to celebrate."

"Are you sure?" said Oscar. "We haven't been there since before Dad—"

The light in the intersection ahead suddenly turned from green to red, skipping yellow altogether, as if something had happened to its sense of order and time. His mother slammed on the brakes, and the Corolla skidded to a halt.

"Crazy," muttered his mom, craning her neck to stare up at the light.

"I mean—" began Oscar, and stopped. He hadn't meant to bring his father up. It had just slipped out. But it was true; they hadn't dined at Rossini's since his dad had left home.

And Rossini's was the place where the three of them used to celebrate.

Birthdays, holidays, and the time when Oscar got the part of Christmas Present in *A Christmas Carol*. Mr. Rossini, short and round, served wine for the adults and bubbly water for the kids. Mr. Rossini's menu featured five kinds of spaghetti. At Mr. Rossini's, the servers were all opera singers from Philadelphia who waited tables on their days off to earn money to pay their rent and, in addition to that, just plain loved singing so much they surrounded your table while you enjoyed your dessert to serenade you in Italian. And Mr. Rossini kept his restaurant open until eleven every night, brightly lit and full of music, even when thunderstorms raged outside. It was truly a place of celebration.

The last time they'd visited had been Oscar's eleventh birthday party. When the singers sang "Happy Birthday," Oscar's mom had taken the high part. And performed it more beautifully than the opera stars. Mr. Rossini had even said he would hire her to work there, if she applied.

And Oscar had always remembered the way her eyes lit up at the thought. The hope, as she gazed around at the beauty and the bustle, that she might be part of it all. His mother felt about singing the way he felt about baseball.

But then his dad had left them only a few days later to chase a dream. He'd explained it all to Oscar: The dream wasn't more important than his family, he'd said. It was just different. He wanted to start his own company. It would be big, located in several countries, stretching worldwide. Which was why he had to leave Oscar and his mom to achieve it. And although the last part didn't really make sense to Oscar, he tried his best to understand.

This had happened a year ago, and ever since, Oscar's mother had grown quiet and started working as a cashier at the gas station during the day and a waitress in a café in the evening. There had been nothing more to celebrate, and Oscar was still waiting for her to take Mr. Rossini up on his offer and apply to work at his fabulous restaurant, but he'd started to lose hope.

"The Wildcats lead the championship series," his mom said admiringly, breaking Oscar out of his reverie. "Wow. Just wow. Of course we have to go to Rossini's!" She parked her wheezing Corolla in front of the restaurant's plate glass window, which was sheeted with rainwater, adorned with three-foot-high, fire-engine-red letters edged in gold, shining in the midst of East

Mt. Etna's gloom: *Rossini's.*

"Only—the thing about Rossini's—right now—" she began, and fell silent.

Oscar heard the catch in her voice, and he saw her eyes dart toward the BBT Bank ATM in the wall next door to the restaurant.

Spaghetti marinara at Rossini's cost fourteen dollars. Two orders cost twenty-eight. Oscar and his mom didn't have much money.

His mom's eyes traveled toward the dashboard of the Corolla. "See if there are any quarters in the ashtray," she instructed.

"Maybe we can just get a pizza," said Oscar, nonchalantly digging for coins. "To go." Rossini's had takeout. A large cheese pie cost $9.99. Breadsticks cost $1.59. "We can call it in right now. And enjoy it at home." Not too many coins to be found. A few pennies and a nickel or two. A couple of quarters mired in some ancient gum. Two dollars and twelve cents, total.

"No!" said his mother. "This is your big night! This is what you've been waiting for!"

Actually, though, the more Oscar thought about it, the more he had to admit that this *wasn't* his big night.

Because his real, live, bona fide big night featured a *true* home run. Not one he'd "hit" with time frozen. Not one he was afraid to tell his mother about. He felt the watch ticking in his pocket.

Actually, this wasn't the night he'd been waiting for *at all.*

"Mom," Oscar said, "I'm not that hungry. Maybe we could just order breadsticks to go. In fact, that's kind of how I'd prefer to celebrate, if you don't mind." He could see Steve Brinkley and his mom and dad inside the restaurant, on the far side of the rain-streaked glass, installed in a corner booth, asking their waiter for spectacular things.

"If you really want to," said his mom, doing her best to hide her relief. "I guess that's all right."

"I really want to," said Oscar.

"I'll order from here and you can run inside when they're ready," said his mom, digging her phone out of her purse.

Oscar got soaked sprinting inside to pick up the breadsticks. And the paper bag got soaked when he ran back out to the car. So did the breadsticks. He set them on the dashboard to dry.

Oddly, at the very moment his mother pulled out of the parking lot, the rain stopped. Completely. As if somebody in the stratosphere had turned off a spigot. Nineteen seconds later, give or take, the moon and stars reappeared.

Oscar and his mother rolled down the windows of the Corolla and belted "We Are the Champions" at the top of their lungs. Oscar's contribution sounded more like howling, truth be told. But his mom sang, really sang, and people at stoplights cocked their ears to listen. At least one good thing had come from stopping time: his mother was singing again, and Oscar couldn't help feeling good about that.

Later that night, Oscar stood in his backyard watching the moon dangle above the trees. He thought about the amazing fact that it didn't appear to move at all, while at the same time it blazed around Earth at a speed of 2,288 miles per hour. Dr. Soul leaped onto the porch railing beside him and contemplated the night, too.

Oscar picked up his old splintery practice bat and imagined a baseball diamond stretching out before him in the darkness of his yard, reaching from his back porch to the edge of Tuscarora Woods. He put ghost runners on the bases, the kind you use to hold your place while you take your next turn at bat. And he put make-believe opponents in the field. They wore the uniform of the old-timey Boston Braves, which was weird, because they were in his imagination and up until that moment, Oscar hadn't known what a Boston Braves uniform even looked like. The players shimmered eerily, like specters. Oscar shuddered. It was getting a little spooky out there.

"I thought things would be different, Dr. Soul," said Oscar, shaking off his shivers. "I thought when I finally hit a home run and won the big game, life would change. I thought I would finally know what it feels like to be a baseball hero. But I blew it. I'm still just Oscar Indigo."

With his bat, Oscar swatted an imaginary home run. Almost. Because one of the ghostly outfielders, who seemed slightly more real than the rest, managed to leap up and snatch it out of the air before it cleared the fence. A surprise feat!

Dr. Soul said nothing in reply to Oscar's lament, of course, but as he gazed at Oscar, absentmindedly licking his rear paw and rubbing his ear with it, Oscar knew what he was thinking: *How would you know hitting a home run didn't change anything? You didn't hit one.*

"You've got a point," Oscar murmured.

And the look Dr. Soul gave in reply was: *Besides, I wouldn't be so sure nothing has changed.* He turned his attention toward the talented outfielder, who glanced over his shoulder and disappeared into the woods.

The moon still seemed to hang motionless in the sky (although of course it must have moved). Inside, Oscar's mother crooned softly to herself. No happy songs this time, nothing about champions. She sang a tune she'd made up herself, one that had no words but was more beautiful because of that, like a whippoorwill singing its lonely song in the empty night.

Later, inside the quiet house, Dr. Soul leaped onto Oscar's bed, stalked across the covers, curled up on Oscar's chest, set himself on "purr," and fell asleep.

Oscar clutched the watch in his fist beneath his pillow—because something told him it'd be a good idea to know exactly where it was at all times—and he promised himself he'd take it back to Eleanor Ethel Ellington first thing in the morning and ask her politely never to give him anything like it ever again.

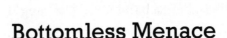

Bottomless Menace

The next morning dawned cool and clear, awash in light, and in it, an angel sang.

A breeze whispered through Oscar's window screen. Squirrels skittered along backyard branches. The sun floated in the sky like a tangerine bubble. One white cloud drifted near the horizon, slowly molding itself into different shapes but never quite taking the form of anything Oscar recognized.

And all across East Mt. Etna, citizens awoke to a new day, a day of pride and promise, because for the first time in history, the East Mt. Etna Wildcats had stomped the sawdust out of the West Mt. Etna Yankees.

Dr. Soul was nowhere to be seen. Oscar figured he must've gotten up early. He did that sometimes.

Once Oscar awoke all the way, the angel's voice turned

out to be his mother's, emanating from the kitchen along with the aroma of pancakes.

He slipped out of bed and padded toward the hall, glancing out his window on the way. He froze. In the bright morning light, there seemed to be a baseball player standing in Oscar's backyard at the shady edge of Tuscarora Woods. A bit ghostly, a bit shimmery. Oscar recognized him. He was the one who'd stolen Oscar's imaginary home run the night before. He still sported the uniform of the long-gone Boston Braves. Oscar stared. The Brave stared back. Then he stepped into the shadows and vanished.

And Oscar blinked and told himself this ghostly ball-player must've been left over from a dream that hadn't quite ended before he woke up.

In the kitchen, Oscar's mom clattered so many utensils together at once, it sounded like a Kindermusik jam session. "What's going on?" Oscar asked. "Why are we having pancakes? How come you're so vivacious?"

"You! You hit a home run!" said his mom. "You're a bona fide bottomless menace!"

"Deep threat, Mom," said Oscar. "Not bottomless menace. When you're a dangerous home-run hitter, people call you a 'deep threat.' But I appreciate the pancakes."

"Why didn't you tell me about it last night?" asked his mother.

"Well. I told you about the part where the Wildcats won," mumbled Oscar. "That's what really matters."

"If you say so," replied his mom. "Have a look at this." She cued a video and slid her phone across the table.

Oscar took the phone. *Ninth Inning Hero*, read the tagline beneath a still of his own face. In the image, he teetered precariously over home plate and peered hopefully into the future. "You're going viral, Oscar!" exclaimed his mother. "Isn't it great?"

"Somebody filmed it on their phone," croaked Oscar. "Wow. That *is* great."

It was awful.

People across town, across the county, state, country, and world were at that very moment watching what he'd done the night before.

For the love of Henry Aaron.

His mom started the video.

"A boy, a dream, a moment in history, a very long shot."

The voice sounded familiar.

"An injured star, a last-minute substitution, a bench

warmer's dream come true."

The voice sounded *very* familiar.

"Undaunted by a lifetime of obscurity, frustration, and failure, Oscar Indigo, of East Mt. Etna, Pennsylvania, overcame years of disappointment tonight."

"That was a little harsh," muttered Oscar. Had he really been that bad?

"Despite a fundamental lack of the basic skills of baseball, Oscar Indigo finally found success at 9:13 p.m. yesterday . . ."

As the narrator spoke, Oscar's at-bat played on video. Taser blew two pitches by him. He didn't seem to have a chance. And then came the final pitch. Right over the plate. The video seemed to stutter and skip. Suddenly, the ball was dropping over the fence. And the crowd went wild.

". . . when he sent the hopes and dreams of his teammates sailing upward into the blackest of nights."

Suzy Armando's face appeared on the screen, smiling at her audience, to close the sequence.

"Wait," muttered Oscar. "That can't be right! Suzy Armando of CSPN? I only *imagined* she was there last night. What's going on?"

"Maybe somebody sent her the video of your home

run, and she liked it enough to do a story on it," said Oscar's mom.

"Maybe," said Oscar. He really hoped this explained it. Because otherwise, things had just gotten really, really weird.

Outside, a flock of towhees swarmed from a bush.

"Hey. I'm applying to Rossini's," said his mom. "Your heroics inspired me! I downloaded the application. I'm filling it out tonight after work. I think 'Summertime' will be my audition tune."

"Fantastic, Mom," said Oscar distractedly. "I'm glad I inspired you."

"You sure did! A home run!" Oscar's mother made her way to the table with three pancakes on a stainless-steel spatula, and he moved his plate so she could reach it, but at that moment, she tried to slide the pancakes off the spatula where the plate had been, so he scooted the plate back; but by then she'd aimed at the spot where he'd moved the plate before he moved it back, and their intentions were good, but their timing was bad, and Oscar's pancakes plopped onto the floor.

"What a disaster," observed his mom cheerfully. "Better clean it up! Oh, my goodness!" she cried, glancing out the window. "Here comes the bus! I have to catch it. The Corolla's battery is dead. I need to buy a new one when I get paid this afternoon. See you tonight!" And with that, she banged out the door.

"Bye, Mom," replied Oscar quietly.

Oscar watched his mom through the window, sprinting to beat the bus to its stop. And then out of nowhere the floor of the kitchen seemed to turn fluid, and its surface seemed to roll away from him in waves. He blinked. He felt dizzy. The roar of the bus outside didn't match the sight of it pulling away from the stop, and inside, the fluttering shadows on the floor didn't match the drifting curtains in the windows. When he stacked his glass and his silverware on his plate to carry it all to the dishwasher, he picked the pile up before it was balanced, and everything slid in different directions. He made a grab for the glass, but he felt like he'd fallen into a YouTube video that hadn't loaded right, where every movement had gone herky-jerky. The glass fell one direction, the silverware another, and it all ended up on the floor, some of it in shards.

The flock of towhees whirred past the window again, this time headed in the other direction. Except for one,

which fluttered backward across the yard, only disappear-
ing into the woods after approximately nineteen seconds
of reverse flying.

"That," said Oscar to himself, "cannot be good."

As soon as he'd cleaned up the mess, Oscar fished
the watch from his pajama pocket and contemplated its
face, huge and pearlescent, with the solid-gold hour and
minute hands, the bright-red sweep hand, and bold black
numbers painted around the dial.

He flipped it over and studied the swirling patterns
adorning the back, and saw words he hadn't seen before:

> *"The time has come," the Walrus said,*
> *"To talk of many things:*
> *"Of shoes—and ships—and sealing-wax—*
> *Of cabbages—and kings—*
> *And why the sea is boiling hot—*
> *And whether pigs have wings."*

Curiouser and curiouser, Oscar thought, and put the
watch in his pocket. He stood up. He knew the time had
come to walk next door and ask Miss Ellington what the
heck was up with this watch. But before he could take
a single step, a pounding erupted at his front door. His

heart beat in his throat. Those men. The ones in the black car! They must have found him! They'd come for him!

Frantically, Oscar opened his mother's bread box and slid the watch inside a hamburger bun, but not before another phrase leaped out at him from its back: *Time is out of joint.*

That seemed like a warning.

The pounding on the door continued.

Carefully, Oscar crept down his hallway and peeked through the tiny peephole.

And spied . . . Lourdes Mangubat?

"Oscar!" she yelled. "Are you in there?" Oscar was shocked. This was more than she'd said to him in the entire time he'd known her.

Mr. Llimb and Mr. Skerritt

Oscar opened the door cautiously. Lourdes stood on his porch staring at him. She balanced on one foot. A rusty old bike leaned against the railing.

Oscar stared back at her. In the silence, the bees in the bee bush next to the porch buzzed maniacally, like they always did, working hard to make life better for everything and everybody: honey, pollination, and just plain sweetness was their contribution.

"My toe—" began Lourdes, interrupting the buzz in Oscar's ears.

"I know," said Oscar.

"I came to tell you—" said Lourdes.

"I'm sorry!" interrupted Oscar. "I'm sorry I spilled OscarAde and made you smash your toe. Does your toe still hurt? I guess you're standing on one foot because your toe still hurts. I feel terrible. Horrible. Awful."

"Actually, I came to tell you it's not so bad," said Lourdes quickly, probably because she wanted to interrupt him before he could start babbling again.

"Wow! That's great news!" Oscar changed gears fast. "Because boy, did I feel atrocious when I did it."

"But you saved the day anyway," said Lourdes. "You hit a home run. Nobody believed you could. Except you. That was kind of awesome."

"Oh. Awesome. Sure. It's awesome when anybody hits a home run. I mean, it was awesome when I did it because I've never even gotten a hit before, but it's also awesome when you do it, because you always get a hit, so it's awesome in a different way—"

Oscar knew he was babbling, and had just said the word *awesome* about a million times, many of them in reference to himself, which most people would not consider cool, but he couldn't stop. It was times like these he wished somebody would please explain to him what was happening in his life. Oddly, a voice in his head began to do just that.

Lourdes Mangubat is a mysterious girl, Suzy. Up till now, nobody has heard her talk this much.

What? Oscar glanced into the front shrubbery. Where had Vern come from? Vern only appeared in his imagination at Wildcats games! Never at his own home. Before he could get his mind around the appearance of Vern, Suzy piped up.

Let's hope Oscar can draw the right conclusion about Lourdes, Vern.

Suzy, if we gather together the observations of many young persons in the greater Mt. Etna area, basic facts emerge: Lourdes Mangubat moved here at the beginning of last school year.

And she appears to make straight As in school, Vern, according to sources who peek over her shoulder when the teacher hands tests back.

Some of her teammates think she could be the first female pitcher in Major League Baseball, Suzy. I guess you could say she's pretty good for a—

Don't even say it, Vern.

Sorry, Suzy.

Actually, Oscar didn't find their commentary all that helpful.

"Your homer was so great," said Lourdes, interrupting his thoughts. "I hardly even minded the smashed toe."

Oscar checked to see if she was joking. It was impossible

to tell. Her face remained perfectly serious.

"Sorry I left without telling you good game last night," said Lourdes. "But if I miss the bus, I have to wait forty-five minutes for the next one."

"That's OK," replied Oscar. "Nobody really expects you to say much. Wait. I'm sorry. That didn't come out right. It's just—you usually don't talk. You're always kind of quiet in the dugout."

"I know. But I wanted to congratulate you. And maybe ask how you hit your homer, since you haven't gotten a single hit all season," replied Lourdes.

"I, ah, yeah," said Oscar. "It's kind of hard to explain."

"That's OK," said Lourdes. "I'm not in a hurry. I mean, I really admire people who don't have any hope of succeeding, but try their best anyway. Like you."

"Wow, thanks," said Oscar, a little stung, but trying not to feel offended. He studied her face. She didn't look like she meant to hurt his feelings.

"You're welcome," said Lourdes. "So. What's your secret, Hank Aaron?"

"OK," began Oscar, thinking fast about how he was going to explain that homer without revealing how badly he'd cheated to make it happen. "This is how it went down," he went on. Then he paused. He found himself stuck. He could say he'd been practicing? But that wasn't right. He could claim it had just been a colossal stroke of good luck? No luck about it, though. . . .

But then he got off the hook, in a really unfortunate way. Taser Tompkins chose that moment to lumber around the corner of Oscar's house. Oscar was slightly glad to see Taser, because now he didn't have to answer Lourdes's question, but on the other hand, nobody ever fainted with joy when Taser Tompkins made the scene.

"Awww," sneered Taser, looking them up and down. "Isn't this sweet? Team bonding, or whatever."

"What are you doing here?" asked Oscar. "How do you even know where I live?"

"Where else would a loser like you live?" shot back Taser, staring in contempt at the small houses and dented cars on Jennifer Street, which indeed must've looked pretty shabby compared to the mansionland he inhabited in West Mt. Etna.

"What do you want?" Oscar demanded.

"To show you what happens to people who make fun of me," said Taser. "Robocop!" he called over his shoulder. "Bring those kumquats!"

Around the corner struggled Robocop Roberts, Taser's faithful sidekick and backup pitcher. He lugged a bucket full of unripe tomatoes from Miss Ellington's garden.

"Taser!" said Oscar. "Those are tomatoes. They're still green. They belong to Miss Ellington. You shouldn't have picked them!"

"Well, we did," gloated Taser.

"They were important to Miss Ellington," said Oscar. And to him, although he managed to keep himself from saying this. "And now they're going to shrivel up and die."

Robocop, always on the lookout for new and creative ways to hurt people, grinned nastily at the success he and Taser had achieved by robbing Miss Ellington, and Oscar realized that ripping the green tomatoes off the bushes must have been his idea.

Calmly, Robocop reached into the bucket and hurled a tomato at Oscar. As when Miss Ellington had thrown the watch at him, he had no time to think—only to react. And he surprised himself by popping his left hand up like a gold-glove first baseman and catching it without leaving so much as a bruise on the green flesh. Carefully, he set the tomato on the grass. Maybe if he put it on his windowsill to ripen later, it would be OK.

"Nice catch," whispered Lourdes, sounding a little surprised. Oscar tipped an imaginary cap at her. He was surprised, too. But he had to save that tomato.

In the meantime, Taser had grabbed another tomato in each hand, and fired them both at Lourdes. She caught them like the champ that she was. Robocop let one fly at Oscar. In the blink of an eye, Oscar caught it in his left hand, and nabbed the next tomato in his right. Six seconds later, the bucket was empty and the tomatoes lined the grass at Oscar's and Lourdes's feet.

"Look," said Lourdes. "All the kumquats are safe! Nice work, Oscar!" And then she whispered to Oscar, "I know they're actually tomatoes. But I don't want to confuse Taser."

"Shut up!" cried Taser, clearly frustrated that the tomato plan had fallen flat. He leaped at Lourdes and twisted her arm behind her.

"You better let go of me," warned Lourdes, "or you'll regret it."

"OK," said Taser. He released Lourdes's arm. And squeezed her skull. Oscar saw her knees wobble.

"Ha!" cried Robocop.

"Come on, Taser, she didn't do anything!" pleaded Oscar.

"Yeah, but you did, and *she'll* keep getting what's coming to *you* until I find out what it was."

"What are you talking about?" asked Oscar.

"Something's not right," said Taser.

"You're no good," said Robocop.

"You can't even get a hit, much less smack a home run," said Taser.

"Especially not off Taser," said Robocop.

"You pulled some kind of fast one," said Taser.

"What are they talking about, Oscar?" wheezed Lourdes.

"Shut up," said Taser. "Oscar knows what we're talking about."

"I'm *not* going to shut up!" said Lourdes. "Let me go!"

Despite the dread rising in Oscar's chest, he couldn't help noticing that being attacked by Taser and Robocop had made Lourdes even more talkative than ever.

"Well?" Taser looked at Oscar as he wrapped his left arm around Lourdes's throat and began squeezing with his right. Lourdes's hand-to-hand combat tactics didn't seem to be as finely honed as her baseball skills, although it was hard to say, since Taser wasn't fighting fair, and she could barely stand on her left foot because of her smashed pinky toe. "I can't breathe," wheezed Lourdes.

"Good," Taser said. "Maybe you'll be quiet."

Lourdes struggled against Taser.

Oscar tried to bean him with the empty tomato bucket

but missed by a foot. "She didn't do anything. Let her go!" demanded Oscar.

Taser ignored this demand, but in the meantime, Lourdes did a backbend, slipped from his grasp, and shook herself free.

"Pretty good," Taser began. "For a—"

"Don't say it!" cried Lourdes.

"For a—"

"I'm telling you—"

"Pretty good for a girl!" Taser sneered.

"Never, ever say that to me," said Lourdes, balling her fists.

Robocop looked at her with his perfectly black eyes, enjoying her rage. "Don't get all mad," he jeered. "He was just paying you a compliment."

Lourdes knocked Taser down like he was made of sticks. Leaping on top of him, her knee in his breadbasket, she drew her fist back and—

"Not good," said a voice like a rat trap snapping. One of the men in black from Miss Ellington's house materialized in Oscar's yard. The small one. In a flash, his hand snaked out and trapped Lourdes's fist. "No hitting. Use your words."

"Who are you?" demanded Lourdes. "Let go of me!"

Oscar glanced over his shoulder to see the giant black car parked at the curb. The other man, the refrigerator-size one, sat behind the wheel.

"Who I am is not important," said the man. "Let Mr. Manners up."

Taser stood up and sidled next to Robocop. "All I said was—" he began to whine.

"I heard what you said," replied the man in black. "And I think maybe it was not a sincere compliment."

"No! I was trying to be nice!" protested Taser.

"Then you're not very good at it," said the man. "You and your friend scram. I need to have a conversation with my pal here. Oscar. That's your name, right? Oscar?" The man draped his arm around Oscar.

Oscar nodded.

"I don't have to scram," objected Taser. "I don't have to do what you say."

The small man in the suit walked back to Taser and cocked his forefinger against his thumb. He flicked Taser's earlobe. "Ow!" cried Taser. "You can't do that!"

"I believe I just did," said the man. He leaned close to Taser and asked, "Are you a loose end?"

"Huh?" said Taser in bewilderment.

"Are you a complication?" a deep voice asked. The

tall man had suddenly joined the conversation. He'd left the car running behind him with his door open, as if he wanted to be able to make a quick escape.

"Are we a what?" snapped Robocop.

"My partner and I don't like loose ends," the tall man said. "Or complications. Get out of here before we have to snip you right out of this caper. *Snip snip.*" He grabbed Taser by the shirt. He made a motion like scissors with his fingers, right in front of Taser's nose.

Taser opened his mouth, but no sound emerged.

"What, no snappy comeback?" asked the small man.

"Come on, Taser," said Robocop, dragging his friend down the sidewalk by his elbow and casting one last glance back at the group. "Let's get out of here. These guys are losers."

"We're not done with you, Indigo," muttered Taser darkly. "We'll be back."

"Let us know when you're dropping by, and we'll bake you a cake," called the short man at Taser's back.

"Allow us to introduce ourselves," said the short man. "I am Mr. Skerritt."

"And I am Mr. Llimb," said the tall one.

"Could we see some ID?" asked Lourdes.

They both fumbled in their jacket pockets and produced laminated security badges.

SMILEY INVESTIGATIVE AGENCY INC., read the badges. ESTABLISHED 1957.

"OK," said Oscar, although he didn't feel totally convinced.

"All right," said Lourdes, sounding none too reassured herself.

"One hundred percent legitimate," said Mr. Llimb as he put his badge back in his pocket. "I made it myself!"

"That's not funny," said Lourdes.

"It's not supposed to be," said Mr. Llimb.

"And now we would like to ask Oscar some questions," said Mr. Skerritt.

"Don't let me stop you," said Lourdes.

"The questions are about a delicate issue that we prefer to keep to ourselves," added Mr. Skerritt. "So if we could respectfully ask you to leave?"

"Leave?" repeated Lourdes.

"Yes," said Mr. Skerritt.

"Do I have to?" protested Lourdes. She seemed surprisingly interested in what the upcoming conversation might hold, for someone who had barely spoken a word in the whole year Oscar had known her. "Oscar?"

"I guess it would be better if you did what these guys ask," said Oscar, remembering the ear flick and the pretend scissors.

Lourdes shrugged, as if she didn't like being disinvited, but OK, whatever, it didn't bother her a whole lot.

Mr. Llimb and Mr. Skerritt waited for her to climb on her bicycle and ride away down the front sidewalk.

And then, turning to Oscar, Mr. Skerritt asked, "All right, Oscar Indigo, what do you know about a watch?"

Oscar noticed that, in the sky, over their fedoras, a jetliner flew. Its contrail stretched out behind it in a zigzag that reached over the horizon, and as he watched, it banked sharply out of a zig and began a zag in the other direction. Which seemed odd.

"What watch?" Oscar asked.

"A watch we've been chasing for a few days now," said Mr. Llimb. "Knocking on doors. Following leads. Hoping for a break."

"I don't think I have the watch you're after," said Oscar.

"With a red button on top to stop time?" said Mr. Skerritt.

"According to our sources, someone pushed it last night," added Mr. Llimb. "This occurrence is believed to have taken place in Mt. Etna. Possibly near the baseball diamond. We heard you had a really remarkable performance on the field last night. So we thought we'd ask you about it."

"Tell us the truth, Oscar," said Mr. Skerritt. "We're professionals. If you don't tell us, we'll find out anyway."

Oscar paused. A part of him had expected someone to come asking about the watch. And he was ready. "I think I put it in my sock drawer," said Oscar, even though he knew it was in the bread box.

"Not there," said Mr. Llimb. "I checked."

"You searched my house?" cried Oscar.

"Just doing our jobs," said Mr. Llimb.

"Maybe I put it under my pillow," murmured Oscar.

"Nope," said Mr. Llimb.

"Did you miss the part where he said to tell the truth?" interrupted Mr. Skerritt.

"OK," sighed Oscar. "It's in the bread box."

"Negative," said Mr. Llimb. "Not there, either."

"What?" said Oscar. "That's where I put it. Fifteen minutes ago. I swear!"

"It's not there now," said Mr. Llimb.

"Then something really strange is going on," said Oscar.

"Couldn't agree more," said Mr. Llimb. He turned toward the car. "If you'll come with us. There's somebody who'd like to talk to you."

Mr. Skerritt must've seen the alarm on Oscar's face. He flashed his badge again. "Nothing to worry about. Just think of yourself as our guest."

"Maybe this isn't a good idea," said Mr. Llimb, slowing his giant automobile as they approached the edge of town, the two men in front, Oscar in the back. Three blocks ahead, a Mt. Etna police cruiser sat at the curb.

"Should we put him in the trunk?" said Mr. Skerritt. He turned to glance over the seat. "You mind riding in the trunk, Oscar? Just until we get out of town? So Mr. Llimb doesn't have to answer any awkward questions?" He pointed at the police car pulling out into traffic.

"Can't you just show the policeman your badges?" asked Oscar.

"The trunk is better for avoiding questions," said Mr. Skerritt.

"It's the most comfortable trunk you ever saw in your life," said Mr. Llimb. "I promise. Very spacious, and we put air holes in it for oxygen circulation and everything."

Ahead, the police car turned left and disappeared around a corner.

"Oh," said Mr. Skerritt. "Look at that. Never mind. Hit it, Mr. Llimb."

Mr. Llimb accelerated smoothly out of town.

Oscar managed to ride silently for a few miles. But soon, his nerves got the better of him. "Where are we going?" he asked. "What's happening? Who are you guys?"

"Like they say in the moving pictures," replied Mr. Llimb, "we're taking you for a ride." He seemed to think this would make Oscar feel better.

"What he means," elaborated Mr. Skerritt, fishing a small, tattered notebook from the depths of his large black suit and consulting it, "is we've been asked to transport you in relative comfort and safety to an unspecified location on Pickwick Island, Delaware. Unspecified to you, I mean. To us, it's specified. We know where we're going."

"You probably said enough, Mr. Skerritt," observed Mr. Llimb. "Where did this cat come from?"

"What cat?" asked Mr. Skerritt.

"This orange cat. The one hiding under my seat," said Mr. Llimb.

Mr. Skerritt reached into the deep, dark footwell of the Cadillac in front of Mr. Llimb and pulled out—

"Dr. Soul?" cried Oscar. Dr. Soul slipped from Mr. Skerritt's grasp, leaped onto Mr. Llimb's shoulder, and catapulted himself over the seat. Mr. Llimb never took his eyes off the road ahead.

"He must've climbed in when I left my door open," said Mr. Llimb.

Dr. Soul rubbed his bony skull against Oscar's knee. He gave Oscar a stare. The stare said, *That's right. I came along to keep you safe. Because obviously you need help with that.*

"Thank you," said Oscar to Dr. Soul.

Somebody sneezed, very softly. "Bless you, Oscar," said Mr. Llimb and Mr. Skerritt in unison.

Which was strange, since Oscar hadn't sneezed. And if neither Mr. Llimb nor Mr. Skerritt had done it, then—

Another muffled sneeze.

"Bless you again," said Mr. Llimb and Mr. Skerritt.

"But I didn't sneeze," said Oscar.

Mr. Llimb looked at him curiously in the rearview mirror. Slowly, he brought the car to a halt on the shoulder of the road.

"Ah-chooo," they heard again.

"Is that coming from the trunk?" said Oscar.

"And while you were talking to Oscar in his yard, I opened the lid and jumped in. There were airholes and everything. It was actually pretty comfortable," said Lourdes as Mr. Llimb, who had found her hiding in the trunk, pulled back onto the highway.

"But why?" asked Mr. Llimb. "Usually, people do everything they can to avoid our trunk."

"Because I asked if I could come," said Lourdes. "And you told me I couldn't."

"Gotta admire your spirit," said Mr. Skerritt. "If not your decision-making."

"Now that I'm here, where are we going?" asked Lourdes.

"Everything will be explained in due time," replied Mr. Llimb, accelerating to ninety-four to pass an ice cream truck blaring "Mary Had a Little Lamb" from the candy-striped speaker on its fudge ripple roof. "Hang on to your cabooses!"

He sawed at the giant black wheel of the Cadillac until its nose pointed down a faded dirt road overrun by all manner of weed and vine. "We're taking a shortcut through the woods!"

"Look. Does that tree have tentacles?" asked Lourdes, startled, as they entered the forest.

"Where?" asked Oscar.

"The one back there," said Lourdes, "behind the Wawa station."

"Probably just your imagination, Lourdes," said Oscar. But it hadn't been. Briefly, he'd also glimpsed the tentacles waving in the summer breeze.

Oscar always tried his best to see a bright side in every situation, but for now, he was stumped. This felt downright scary.

Rogue Wave

"We're here!" sang out Mr. Skerritt as Mr. Llimb wrestled the Cadillac to a halt in the sandy parking lot of Pickwick Island State Seashore.

Oscar, who had fallen into a troubled doze, dreams of tentacled trees writhing around in his brain, opened one eye. He saw an eye looking back at him. He opened his other eye. He saw another eye looking back at him. They both belonged to Lourdes Mangubat, who was leaning close to him.

"We can escape from these guys," whispered Lourdes very quietly. "When we get out of the car, I'll stomp on Mr. Skerritt's toes and trip Mr. Llimb. You run for the lifeguard."

"No whispering in the backseat!" said Mr. Skerritt.

"Actually," said Oscar, "I want to see where they're taking us. I can't explain everything right now, but I kind of need to find out what's going on."

"That could be cool, too," said Lourdes.

"I'm glad you think so," said Oscar.

"Do guys in black show up and take you to the beach very often?" she asked.

"Believe it or not, this is the very first time," replied Oscar.

"Oh. Interesting. You know, I've never actually been to the beach," she said thoughtfully. "Usually, I spend the whole summer at Elite Select pro-development baseball camp. This should be fun."

"Well, the next time men in suits come to take me for a ride," said Oscar, "I'll make sure to call you."

Lourdes giggled.

"What's so funny?" demanded Mr. Skerritt. "Huh?"

"Nothing," replied Oscar.

"A beautiful day at the seashore!" roared Mr. Llimb, stepping out of the car.

"Let's get moving," said Mr. Skerritt. "Kids, bring the cat. Because we would never leave a pet locked in a vehicle on a summer day."

"Last one there is a rotten tomato," added Mr. Llimb, locking the car behind them. "And you know what happens to rotten tomatoes."

"Are you limping?" Mr. Llimb asked Lourdes after a bit. They had crossed the parking lot and were on the sand now. "How come you're limping?"

"My toe hurts," said Lourdes. Oscar glanced at her, embarrassed.

"Let me have a look at it," said Mr. Llimb.

"That's all right—" began Lourdes.

"No. Really. Let me have a look at it," ordered Mr. Llimb.

"OK," said Lourdes.

She sat down and untied her shoe. Mr. Llimb crouched beside her. She slid her foot out and Mr. Llimb had a look. "By golly. It's dislocated!" he said.

"That's my fault," said Oscar miserably. "I'm really sorry, Lourdes."

"We'll take care of it in a jiffy," said Mr. Llimb.

"Really?" asked Oscar.

"This might smart, Lourdes," said Mr. Llimb. "Oscar, get out of the way. Mr. Skerritt, grab her." Mr. Skerritt slid his arms under Lourdes's and hoisted her off the sand. Mr. Llimb held her toe in his fist and pulled. Oscar could swear he saw it stretch out to twice its length, like it was made of rubber. Then Mr. Llimb let it go. With a popping sound, it snapped back into place.

"Wow," whispered Lourdes as Mr. Skerritt lowered her gently to the ground again. "That hurt."

"I figured," said Mr. Llimb. "Lefty Lefkowitz passed out when I performed the procedure on him after the Union Street job. But what was the good in telling you about that beforehand and getting you all worried?"

"Excellent point," muttered Lourdes through clenched teeth.

"Try walking on it now," said Mr. Llimb.

Lourdes cautiously put weight on her foot. She raised her eyebrow. She took a step. She took another. She put her shoe on. She ran to the edge of the parking lot and back. She did a cartwheel. With perfect form, of course. "Hardly hurts at all!" she said. Oscar let out the breath he'd been holding. At least these guys were good for something.

"I got pretty skilled at first aid back in the day," said Mr. Llimb proudly.

"Came in handy, really," added Mr. Skerritt. "What

with all the broken bones we encountered." Before Oscar and Lourdes could think about what that meant, Mr. Llimb set off toward the crowds of beachgoers on the far side of the dune and called, "Come on. Let's get cracking!"

Oscar had a feeling that, like a lot of things he'd witnessed lately, two men in black suits and black hats with their pants rolled up to their knees and their fish-white feet bare amid the splashers, swimmers, Frisbee tossers, and surfers of Pickwick Island Seashore was a sight never before seen by human eyes.

You rarely run across guys dressed like morticians at the beach, and even when you do, they're *never* passing an orange cat back and forth with a couple of kids and constantly saying "Bless you! Bless you!" to one of them, who is sneezing.

But if Mr. Llimb and Mr. Skerritt stuck out, they hardly seemed to notice the stares, and they sure didn't care. They just trudged through the sand wearing their black felt hats, sweating like coal miners, plowing furrows in the beach among the blankets with their big feet.

But two giant men in black weren't the only questionable spectacle on the beach. Oscar noted uncomfortably that things felt slightly off. The laughter of kids and moms and dads darting in and out of the surf rang against the blue sky like the echoes of an alarm bell. The screams of excitement uttered by wave riders fluttered on the edge of hysteria. Arctic terns shrieked as they dove at sandwiches held by toddlers. Unruly clouds seethed overhead as waves churned against one another, and all the while, high-pitched wails echoed against the sky. Oscar wondered what was going on. Maybe the last inscription he'd seen on the watch had been right. Maybe time *was* out of joint. And maybe these people were starting to feel it.

Slowly, the noise and activity began to die down. A strange hush settled over the beach. The waves calmed until the surface of the ocean lay as smooth as glass. Beachgoers stopped what they were doing and turned to look. And then, slowly at first, and then faster and faster, the sea drew away from the shore several feet and then several more, and then more and more and more, until it seemed as if the salt water would recede all the way to Portugal, leaving the ocean floor bare to the horizon.

"Clear the beach!" cried the lifeguards, blowing their whistles frantically.

But there was no time.

Because now the water had stopped retreating. And it was rolling toward the dunes in one giant wave. It moved faster and towered higher as it came. The line of surfers who'd been left stranded started to run. Kids with boogie boards scrambled toward high ground. The mothers and the fathers of the toddlers in floaties grabbed their babies and tried to flee.

But it was happening too fast.

"Oscar, Lourdes, Mr. Skerritt, hold on to me!" cried Mr. Llimb. They did. Luckily, Mr. Llimb was quite large and there was plenty to grab: sleeves, lapels, long black tie.

Just as they all clambered onto Mr. Llimb, the rogue wave crashed across the beach. When it hit, it was six feet high, but it spread out as it rolled in, so soon it was five feet high, and then four, and then three, and then knee-deep, carrying with it folding chairs and umbrellas and ice chests and paperback books and decks of cards and sunglasses and hats and paddleball paddles and skim boards and sunscreen and Mountain Dew bottles and, tumbling over the sand here and there, people. It rolled everything up into a giant froth and washed its load over the dune and across the boardwalk through the changing house and dumped it in the parking lot.

The beach lay deserted in its wake, and Mr. Llimb towered like an oak in the middle of it all, unmoved, with

Lourdes, Oscar, Mr. Skerritt, and Dr. Soul clinging to his suit. The water slid back to the ocean placidly.

Oscar let go of Mr. Llimb and breathed a sigh of relief, because even though a few babies howled, nobody seemed seriously hurt. But he wondered: Had this wave happened because time was out of joint? And was time out of joint because he'd stopped the watch? Could this mayhem be his fault, too?

"Phew, close one! We'd better get this young man to the boss," said Mr. Llimb, wringing the water out of his pants cuffs. "Pronto. Things are changing faster than we thought."

They set off north along the shore.

"Where are we going?" asked Lourdes twenty minutes later as they struggled through the endless sand. "When will we get there?"

"Look. I think that's where we're headed," said Oscar, pointing at a speck in the distance.

Mr. Llimb, Mr. Skerritt, and Lourdes squinted.

"I don't see anything," said Lourdes.

"That man standing by himself on the beach, staring at the waves," said Oscar. "Near the abandoned submarine watchtower."

Silently, the others scanned the sand. Finally, Lourdes said, "I see him. A speck on the shore."

"Gee willikers," said Mr. Skerritt. "Your friend has good eyes."

"When they're open," tossed in Lourdes.

"If you're talking about his batting technique," said Mr. Llimb, "I have to agree."

As they approached the man, Oscar could see he was thin and tanned. From behind a cascade of long, blond bangs, his eyes pondered the waves. He studied each one intently as it broke over the sand. He watched them all crash, and swirl together, and combine into small rivers that flowed back to the sea, and then pull apart and re-form and break again, over and over and over. From time to time, the man smiled a little at what he saw. He seemed to be observing something spectacular in the never-repeating patterns of ocean waves.

"Oscar and Lourdes, allow me to introduce Dr. T. Buffington Smiley," said Mr. Llimb.

"Professor emeritus at Massachusetts Institute of Technology, California Institute of Technology, Rensselaer Polytechnic Institute, and Gloucester County Institute of Technology," added Mr. Skerritt.

"Our boss," concluded Mr. Llimb.

"Pleased to meet you," said T. Buffington Smiley, pulling his blue eyes away from the water to gaze kindly at Oscar and Lourdes.

"Why are we here?" Lourdes demanded.

T. Buffington Smiley blinked at the bluntness of her question. "Mr. Llimb, did I ask you to bring this delightful young woman?" he asked. It didn't sound like he was being a jerk. It sounded like he really wanted to know. It seemed like he honestly couldn't remember if he'd requested Lourdes's presence.

"She kind of invited herself," said Mr. Llimb.

"Under circumstances beyond our control," added Mr. Skerritt.

T. Buffington Smiley turned his face back toward the ocean. He never lost his smile. "How about if we take a moment to contemplate the waves?" he said.

"Maybe," said Lourdes, pointing with a quivering hand to a two-hundred-year-old warship under full sail, carrying men wearing red coats, who peered glumly over the rail as they cruised by, "we should contemplate that antique boat full of British soldiers."

Oscar gazed at the ship in fascination and in dread. It seemed to have sailed in straight from the Revolutionary

War. Time must be way, way out of joint, he realized.

Mr. Llimb and Mr. Skerritt observed the ship and exchanged a rueful glance.

"Right," said T. Buffington Smiley solemnly, as the ship sailed out of sight. "You're exactly right. Things are getting weird. And they're going to get weirder."

"What do you mean? Do you know why these things are happening?" asked Oscar. Fear crept into his voice, though he tried to keep it out.

"I do," said T. Buffington Smiley. "I am a cosmologist. Which means I study the workings of the universe. When I first started, I performed my computations with a pencil and paper. And then I graduated to what is known as a slide rule. Next, to find answers, I punched calculator buttons. And for a while there, when I worked at NASA, I enjoyed using one of the most powerful computers known to man."

"What happened to all your stuff?" asked Oscar.

"Left it at the office when I moved to the beach," said T. Buffington Smiley. "Now I consult the waves, and I draw my conclusions from the unpredictable but meaningful interactions of their swirls."

"Is that a new technique?" asked Lourdes dubiously.

"Yes," replied T. Buffington Smiley. "I am the first

and only scientist in the world to use it. So far. But it could catch on." A breaker crashed near their feet. It shot up the sand further than the one before. "A new sun," said T. Buffington Smiley finally, "is lifting the tides. More every day."

"What new sun?" asked Lourdes.

"A rogue star out there," said Professor Smiley, waving at the heavens. "Caught in the gravitational field of our solar system. I can see its influence in the patterns of the waves. I calculate that it came within nineteen seconds of passing us safely by. But last night, there was a glitch in time, and nineteen seconds went missing at exactly the wrong moment. Now the star is caught in our solar system's pull and approaching us. Soon, astronomers will detect it, and after that, it will become a second sun in our sky."

"How do you know about the rogue star, if astronomers haven't detected it yet?" asked Oscar, his unease growing, especially at the mention of the nineteen-second glitch, which he was pretty sure he was responsible for, since who else had caused a nineteen-second hiccup in time except for him?

"I have observed the star's pull on the sea," said

T. Buffington Smiley, gesturing at the endless waves. "I have traced the movements of the waves and the tides all the way into to space, to confirm the rogue star's existence."

"So what do we do?" asked Oscar.

T. Buffington Smiley raised one finger and observed the sea as it ebbed away again. "I, personally, will do what I always do, which is watch for the wave that tells me the answer."

Before them, the ocean heaved forward, and a towering swell sped toward the sand, lifting the gray surface of the water like the back of an enormous beast, until it reared, tipped, and broke with a roar, darting in a foamy sheet up the beach to inundate their feet. "That one was almost as big as the one that wiped out all the picnic blankets," observed Mr. Skerritt.

As the wave receded, with flecks of quartz and pearlescent shells flashing in its wake, the next roller tripped over it, thudding onto the sand, causing the whole beach to reverberate like a hollow floor pounded by a thousand boot heels. It slid back down shore, only to be devoured by the next wave.

And something about this enormous breaker snapped

T. Buffington Smiley out of his reverie. He turned to Mr. Llimb and Mr. Skerritt. "Maybe you two can take the cat for a walk. Lourdes, too."

"I'b allergic to cats," said Lourdes, sneezing at the mere mention of a stroll with Dr. Soul.

"No," said T. Buffington Smiley, regarding her thoughtfully. "You're not. Cats just make you nervous. Take a deep breath. Relax. Visualize Dr. Soul's silky orange fur and his mesmerizing green eyes. Ponder the mystery that is *the cat*."

Lourdes cocked an eyebrow as if to say *I know this won't make me stop sneezing*, but she didn't protest. Dr. Soul picked his way across the damp sand and rubbed himself around her ankles.

"How do you feel?" asked T. Buffington Smiley.

"About the sabe, so far," replied Lourdes doubtfully, but she followed Dr. Soul, Mr. Llimb, and Mr. Skerritt along the beach anyway.

"Now," said T. Buffington Smiley, turning his attention to Oscar when the others were out of earshot, "we need to talk about the watch."

"I—I know," said Oscar.

"Many very powerful people want that watch back where it belongs," said T. Buffington Smiley. "They have enlisted me and my friends Mr. Llimb and Mr. Skerritt to help. I do most of the thinking. Mr. Llimb and Mr. Skerritt knock on doors and track down leads."

"Who wants the watch back, Professor Smiley?" asked Oscar.

"The FBI, the CIA, the Pentagon, NASA, the Smithsonian Institution, the Franklin Institute in Philadelphia, and the Veeder-Klamm Thimble and Handheld Timepiece Museum of Mt. Etna," said T. Buffington Smiley. "For starters."

"Wow. Those places are all pretty good at finding things. Why did they need your help?" asked Oscar.

"Because I'm even better at locating lost items than they are," said T. Buffington Smiley. "Partly because I have colleagues like Mr. Llimb and Mr. Skerritt, who are skilled at searching door to door. Partly because I know the right questions to ask. And now, I have to ask *you* one of those questions. And I hope you will answer honestly. Do you have the watch hidden where Mr. Llimb and Mr. Skerritt can't find it?"

"No," said Oscar.

"*Did* you have the watch?" asked T. Buffington Smiley.

"Yes!" said Oscar. Just admitting this made him feel a million times better.

"Would you mind telling me how you got it?" asked T. Buffington Smiley.

"My neighbor gave it to me," said Oscar. "Miss Ellington."

"Does she by any chance ride a giant tricycle?" asked T. Buffington Smiley. "Because Mr. Llimb and Mr. Skerritt have been searching Mt. Etna for the rider of a giant tricycle who was caught on security camera footage around the time the watch disappeared from its tamperproof, fireproof, bombproof vault in the basement of the Veeder-Klamm Thimble and Handheld Timepiece Museum, which for years has been its rightful home."

"She does have a trike like that," said Oscar. "But Miss Ellington would never steal anything. I don't know how the watch got on her kitchen table. She said I could have it as a token of appreciation for helping water her tomatoes. Which was weird. Because she never gives me a token of appreciation for helping water her tomatoes . . . except for maybe some hot chocolate." When he finished, Oscar felt like he could breathe for the first time since he'd fabricated his homer. He hadn't realized how badly he needed to tell somebody about everything that'd happened. "Men were knocking on her door—Mr. Llimb and Mr. Skerritt, even though I didn't know who they were at the time. I guess Miss Ellington wanted to get the watch out the back of the house before they came in the front. But after she gave it to me, I think I made a mistake."

"Which was?" asked T. Buffington Smiley.

"I used it to stop time. So I could hit a home run," said Oscar, staring at his feet in the sand.

"I see. And how long did you keep time stopped?" asked T. Buffington Smiley.

"Eighteen seconds," said Oscar. "Nineteen, if you add the second when my mom was yelling at me about my socks."

"Anything else you want to get off your chest?" asked T. Buffington Smiley.

"Yes," said Oscar. "After I used the watch, I put it in the bread box for safekeeping. But it disappeared!"

"Wow," said T. Buffington Smiley. "A rapidly escalating catastrophe."

"What's going on, Professor Smiley?" Oscar blurted. "Is there more to the story? I did something terrible, didn't I? That's why there was a miniature tsunami at Pickwick Island Seashore. That's why the trees have tentacles. That's why there are pterodactyls in the sky."

"Yes," T. Buffington Smiley said slowly, "but don't

panic. We may be able to fix this." He paused. "Although it won't be easy."

"All I wanted was for the Wildcats to win. It was my fault they were going to lose because I got Lourdes injured. Everyone was counting on me," moaned Oscar. "That's why I used the watch. Oh, I can't believe I did this. Wait. What did I do, exactly?"

"You broke the universe," said T. Buffington Smiley. "There's no other way to put it."

"How could I have done something so terrible?" wailed Oscar.

"Here's how," replied T. Buffington Smiley. "Our universe is part of an infinite collection of universes. Some people think of it as the 'multiverse.' I think of it as a mind-bendingly large tomato plant. This tomato plant is always growing, expanding, budding and branching, sprouting new shoots every nanosecond. And each one of those branches is a universe, and one of those universes is ours."

"Our universe is a branch of a tomato plant?" clarified Oscar.

"A mind-bendingly large, theoretical one, yes," said T. Buffington Smiley. "Always growing as time flows by. I like to imagine that it's planted in the garden of a little old lady who takes very good care of it."

"I know a little old lady like that," blurted out Oscar. "A real one, I mean. With real tomato plants. Sorry I interrupted. Can you tell me more about what I did?"

"Time is like rain falling on the leaves of the plant," continued T. Buffington Smiley. "When time flows, the cosmic plant thrives."

"What if time doesn't flow?" asked Oscar.

"You mean, for instance," asked T. Buffington Smiley, "what if a certain person who I won't name were to halt the fundamental processes of our branch to, I don't know, score a run in a baseball game?"

"Sure," said Oscar. "Let's go with that example."

"Just like the branch of a real tomato plant, when there is no water," said T. Buffington Smiley, "the branch of the cosmic tomato plant shrivels. It droops. It gets a kink in it."

"I only stopped time for nineteen seconds," said Oscar. "How much could that hurt?"

"Possibly a lot," said T. Buffington Smiley. "Those nineteen seconds you took are bouncing around the universe right now like a hand clap in an empty stadium. They're bounding and rebounding and redounding all along the length of our branch, growing more momentous all the time. You took nineteen seconds from yesterday, so yesterday took nineteen seconds from today, and today took nineteen from a day long ago, and that day took nineteen seconds from another day, and so it goes on and on all along the branch."

"Redcoats off the shore of Delaware," said Oscar. "Trees with tentacles. Boston Braves among the ghost runners. And flocks of tiny pterodactyls."

"Those glitches in time make snarls in the universe," T. Buffington Smiley continued.

"What kind of snarls?" asked Oscar.

"Snarls in which good people fail. Bad people succeed. In which your friends and loved ones will experience disappointment and defeat. Your adversaries will enjoy triumph. In which everything falls apart. After a while, if the branch gets gnarled enough, the cosmic little old lady in charge of tending the tomato plant will snap it right off and throw it away."

"This is terrible," whispered Oscar. "What you're saying is awful, even though you did an awesome job explaining it."

"Thank you, little brother, thank you. The clarity of my explanations has contributed greatly to my success in the scientific community. But I have to tell you. The situation is bad. It's getting worse. You have to act fast. You have to fix the disruption you caused."

"What do I do?" asked Oscar.

"Three things," said T. Buffington Smiley, gazing at the waves as if reading them. "One, find the watch before somebody uses it again. We've already lost nineteen seconds. We can't afford to lose any more. Two, put back the nineteen seconds you already took. And three, beat the Yankees fair and square, to make up for the victory you stole. If you don't accomplish all three tasks, our universe is done for."

"Wow. That's a lot to accomplish. Could you by any chance help me?" asked Oscar, panicked by the overwhelming tasks.

"Unfortunately, I can't," said T. Buffington Smiley. "I must remain here by the seaside. Someone needs to keep an eye on the condition of the universe, and that someone is me. I am best suited to doing so here on the beach, where I can watch the ocean waves."

A fitful breeze began to blow across the sand again.

Suddenly, Dr. Soul came tearing out of the dunes. On his tail followed a saber-toothed cat, twenty yards behind but gaining. Every second, the big cat got closer to the little housecat.

"Dr. Soul!" cried Oscar, running toward his pet. But just as the saber-toothed cat prepared to leap, it disappeared in a vortex of windblown sand. Dr. Soul stopped to lick his paws and to shoot Oscar a resentful look.

"Lucky. That enormous beast's moment with us ran out just in time," observed T. Buffington Smiley. "He had to go back where he came from."

Oscar knew without counting that nineteen seconds had passed. A perfect example of *his* time pulling nineteen seconds from *another* time to make up for *lost* time. It was just too bad that the nineteen seconds his time chose happened to have an ancient predator in them.

Just then, Lourdes came running up, with Mr. Llimb and Mr. Skerritt close behind. She scooped Dr. Soul into her arms. "You're safe! Oh, thank goodness." She buried her face in his fur, which appeared to annoy him a little but didn't bother her at all. "Professor Smiley was right," she said. "I'm not allergic! It was just my fear of cats! I'm over it now. There are much scarier felines in the world—did you see that saber-toothed tiger? Dr. Soul's a stuffed animal compared to him! I think Dr. Soul is wonderful. And I'm so glad he's safe!"

"Awwwwww," said Mr. Skerritt, patting Dr. Soul affectionately.

"If the coast is clear, we'd better hit the road," said Mr. Llimb, scanning the beach for any additional prehistoric predators. "Or people back in Mt. Etna are gonna start wondering where these kids are."

"Remember your three tasks, Oscar," said T. Buffington Smiley.

"I'll remember," responded Oscar. "How could I forget?"

Silence filled the Cadillac as they drove home.

Mr. Llimb and Mr. Skerritt seemed to be occupied by thoughts of their own, and Dr. Soul embarked on what would turn out to be a two-hour nap, which was actually kind of short, by his standards. Lourdes and Oscar sat quietly in the backseat.

"I had an interesting time today," said Lourdes, breaking the silence. "I'm glad you didn't get mad when I sneaked into your trunk."

"No problem," said Mr. Llimb, glancing at her in the rearview mirror.

"But I have one thing to ask," Lourdes continued.

"What is it?" asked Mr. Skerritt.

"Can somebody please explain everything that just happened?"

"Sure," said Mr. Llimb.

"Absolutely," said Mr. Skerritt.

"Oscar, go right ahead," said Mr. Llimb.

"Don't mind us, not one bit," said Mr. Skerritt.

"OK. Well. First of all—" began Oscar. And then he stopped. Much like the coffee suspended in the air above his mom's mug, he dangled, neither here nor there, neither up nor down.

"First of all, what?" prompted Lourdes. "Oscar?"

He needed to tell her something. Obviously. But unfortunately, the truth was not an option. For one thing, it involved his cheating at baseball—which he really didn't want to reveal to Lourdes Mangubat, the best baseball player he'd ever known. The truth also involved Oscar's breaking the universe, which was just terrible. Maybe he could get away with only part of the truth? Which part, though? He imagined different lines he might deliver. "I fudged?" No. "The multiverse is a cosmic tomato plant, and I broke the limb we live on?" Didn't exactly have the right ring. "I have to accomplish three impossible tasks?" Sounded like the beginning of a movie with elves in it.

Oscar looked up, flustered. Lourdes was staring at him. "There's a watch!" he burst out finally. "It's missing."

"Professor Smiley lost his watch?" asked Lourdes.

"Yes," said Oscar slowly, feeling Mr. Llimb's and Mr. Skerritt's eyes on him. He knew they knew this wasn't the whole truth, but Oscar blundered on. "Professor Smiley lost his watch."

"Does he need your help to find it or something?" pressed Lourdes.

Oscar hesitated. If he explained any more, he would reveal too much.

"Yes," answered Oscar, simply.

"I could help you find it," said Lourdes. "Uncle Nonoy left his metal detector in Mom's garage. He won't mind if we use it. He won't be back from Manila for three years, at least. The only thing is, if Professor Smiley lost his watch, why are we going back to Mt. Etna? That doesn't make sense. Shouldn't we be looking around Pickwick Island?" When Oscar didn't respond, she asked, "Is there something you're not telling me?"

"Actually," said Oscar, "it's a little complicated. I think it will take more than just a metal detector to find the watch. Professor Smiley isn't exactly sure where to start looking. He asked me to help him think it over."

"I'm good at thinking," Lourdes declared. She stared

straight ahead, but Oscar could see her watching him out of the corner of her eye, waiting for him to ask her to help find the watch. "Want to come to my house tonight after the game and think it over together? We can have a bonfire. In the backyard. With s'mores."

"S'mores always help me think," tossed in Mr. Skerritt.

But after that observation, silence fell.

"So. Do you want to come make s'mores and try to figure out where Professor Smiley's watch is?" Lourdes pressed.

If only the problem were as simple as finding a lost watch, Oscar thought, then sure, he'd have said yes. But he'd lied. Cheated. Broken the universe. That was not so simple. And it was not a problem he wanted to—or even *could*—share with Lourdes. "Thanks," he replied. "But I can't."

"Oh. OK," said Lourdes, sounding stung. "Fine."

"It's just that it's *my* mission. T. Buffington Smiley gave it to me. For a reason," said Oscar. He noticed Mr. Llimb watching him in the rearview mirror, but as soon as he met Mr. Llimb's eyes, Mr. Llimb looked away.

"Really. It's OK. I don't care," replied Lourdes tartly. The look she gave Oscar before turning to stare silently out the window for the remainder of the trip made him feel like he'd just dropped a fly ball in the bottom of the ninth. And that fly ball was Lourdes Mangubat's feelings.

And of all the fly balls he'd dropped so far in his life, this was the one Oscar regretted most.

Mr. Veeder

Putting a merciful end to the smothering silence that'd filled the car since the thoughtful but disastrous s'mores invitation, Mr. Llimb and Mr. Skerritt dropped Lourdes off at her house, which had pretty flowers in the yard.

Then they drove along the edge of Tuscarora Woods to Oscar's home.

"We'll see you around, kid," said Mr. Skerritt as they rolled to a stop in his driveway.

"Yeah, we'll give you regular news updates from Professor Smiley," added Mr. Llimb.

"Thanks for the ride, Mr. Llimb and Mr. Skerritt," said Oscar.

"I wish everybody we kidnapped was as polite as you," said Mr. Llimb.

"And hey, kid, don't take things so serious-like," said Mr. Skerritt. "Yeah, sure, you got yourself mixed up in something big, something so colossal it might spell the end of existence as we know it, but that doesn't mean you can't make s'mores with your friends once in a while."

"You guys shouldn't eavesdrop on other people's conversations!" cried Oscar.

"Sorry," said Mr. Skerritt. "Old habits die hard. But keep my advice in mind."

"I'll try to do that," said Oscar, hoisting Dr. Soul, who'd made himself into cat jelly in an attempt to slip out of his grasp.

"We're driving down to the headquarters of NASA," said Mr. Skerritt. "To pick up Professor Smiley's surfboard from his old office. Just in case he spots the wave that will reveal what he's looking for and decides to rush into the sea to ride it."

"See ya in the funny papers," added Mr. Llimb.

And the Cadillac roared away in a cloud of blue smoke.

An idea popped into Oscar's mind. In order to find out where the watch was *now*, he thought it might help to learn about where it had *been*. He sprinted around to the back of his house, placed Dr. Soul gently inside, and ran to the garage for his bicycle.

* * *

So what if Oscar's bike was a hand-me-down from his cousin Julia, who'd outgrown it? So what if Julia was only eleven, and the bike was three sizes too small for him? So what if it was pink, with tassels in the handgrips? So what if Julia had left it lying in the driveway and his uncle had backed over the front wheel so it wobbled like it belonged on the last cart in the whole grocery store?

It had only taken Oscar ten seconds to snip off the tassels, three minutes to bang the wheel almost totally round with a wooden hammer, and six more minutes to paint a black stripe around the crossbar, making it look really fast.

And even though one pedal was slightly loose, it *was* fast. Especially going downhill. Riding it, perhaps Oscar might forget for a moment that he'd broken the universe and lost the first real friend he'd made in years and that if he didn't find the watch, everyone he knew would suffer and pay. Riding his bike, Oscar felt free. He felt confident. Sure, he had his work cut out for him, but he was going to fix things. He just knew it.

On his way out of the garage, he listened for bees in the bee bush, but they were gone. Another sign that the universe was collapsing. "Don't worry, bees, wherever you are," said Oscar. "I'm going to fix everything."

He had a plan.

Oscar pedaled along streets of crumbling asphalt and potholes that would flatten his tires and bend his rims if he wasn't careful, right to the middle of town. There, straddling the invisible, imaginary line that divided East Mt. Etna from West Mt. Etna, almost in the shadow of Mt. Etna Diamond, stood the Veeder-Klamm Thimble and Handheld Timepiece Museum. Oscar figured if he needed more information on the mysterious watch he'd just used to destroy the universe, he should trace its whereabouts back to the moment when it disappeared from the museum, its rightful home.

The sign out front read, OPEN 9–5 EVERY DAY. Old Mr. Veeder didn't have much to do besides run his museum, and even when it was closed, he could usually be found there, because he lived on the second floor.

Strangely, though, when Oscar tried the door, it was locked. He knocked.

"We're closed, Oscar," cried Mr. Veeder from inside. "Congratulations on your home run! Now go home."

"You have to let me in," insisted Oscar. "And thanks for the congratulations," he added, although his shoulders sagged a bit, because that home run was really starting to feel like a burden.

"Why do I have to let you in?" asked Mr. Veeder.

"I need information," said Oscar from the front steps.

"About what?" asked Mr. Veeder.

"The watch," said Oscar.

"I have a lot of watches," replied Mr. Veeder. "Thimbles, too. Did you notice the name of the museum?"

"This is a watch you *don't* have," said Oscar. "This is the watch that disappeared from its vault in your basement. This is the watch that halts—"

"Shhhh!" hissed Mr. Veeder, hurriedly opening the door. He glanced up and down the street but saw nobody. "Come inside!" he ordered.

Oscar entered the museum.

"Now, what kind of nonsense are you talking?" demanded Mr. Veeder, closing the door behind Oscar. He was not the most patient man ever to run a museum, and today he seemed even grumpier than usual. Probably, Oscar noted, another sign of the deteriorating universe.

"I want to know about the watch that can stop time," replied Oscar. "The one you used to have locked up for safekeeping?"

"I've been hearing that hogwash for years!" snapped

Mr. Veeder. "There never was such a watch. And even if there was, I never heard of it. And even if I'd heard of it, I certainly never had anything like that stored in a secret vault in my museum. And even if I had something like that stored in a secret vault in my museum, it certainly didn't disappear recently. Why do you ask?"

"It's missing. I'm trying to find it," said Oscar. "I— accidentally—used it."

"Oh my goodness," said Mr. Veeder, and the fight seemed to leak out of him. "You did? I mean, I still claim no such watch exists, but if it did exist, and if it disappeared from my vault, you're saying you activated it?"

"Yes," said Oscar. "I used it last night. And then it disappeared from my bread box this morning."

"Very upsetting," said Mr. Veeder.

"And Professor T. Buffington Smiley says I need to get it back before somebody uses it again," said Oscar.

"Professor Smiley is right. You do need to get that watch back, pronto, before somebody else uses it," agreed Mr. Veeder, finally admitting he knew what Oscar was talking about.

"I want to find it more than anything in the universe," said Oscar, "but I don't even know where to start. Can you help me, Mr. Veeder?"

"The story of that watch is classified. Top secret," said Mr. Veeder. "Only highly placed government officials, special investigators, and certain museum directors are supposed to know about it. So no. I can't tell you."

"Mr. Veeder," said Oscar, "the fate of the universe is at stake. I know I look like just a kid to you, and I am, but the thing is, I'm the kid who made a cosmic mistake last night, and I'm also the kid who is going to fix that mistake."

Mr. Veeder silently contemplated Oscar's declaration. After a long pause, he said, "These are extraordinary circumstances, and I believe they justify breaking the rules. Oscar, that watch is one of the most powerful scientific devices ever invented. You must know that, if you've already spoken to Professor Smiley. The watch is so powerful, it is dangerous. So dangerous, it was banished to an uncrackable vault in this very museum in this very obscure town where nobody would ever think to look for it. And it's stayed here ever since, in the Veeder-Klamm Thimble and Handheld Timepiece Museum."

"Who would make such a powerful and dangerous watch?" asked Oscar.

"A man who wanted to save the world," said Mr.

Veeder. "A brilliant one. His name was Hector Smiley."

"Is he related to T. Buffington Smiley?" asked Oscar.

"Indeed, he was T. Buffington Smiley's great-uncle," said Mr. Veeder.

"No wonder Professor Smiley is so smart," said Oscar. "But if this Smiley guy was so brilliant, why did he make such a watch?"

"Well, let me tell you, the smartest ideas don't always lead to the best results." Here Mr. Veeder looked pointedly at Oscar and Oscar shifted uncomfortably, thinking about his homer. Mr. Veeder continued, "The watch began as a wonderful idea. An idea meant to save the world. . . ."

The Story of the Watch, as told by Mr. Veeder
April 7, 1935

After years of intently observing the secrets of the universe and studying the discoveries of Albert Einstein, Werner Heisenberg, and Ludwig Boltzmann, Hector Smiley invented an ingenious contraption of wires and switches that could freeze time completely, while leaving him to move freely outside of it.

He managed to fit his invention into a standard

gold railroad watch, though he replaced the gold button on top with one that glittered red for stop, green for go.

He theorized that his discovery might turn out to be the ultimate force for good, a means of halting any menace that might threaten, a way of stopping catastrophes before they started, a tool for reversing calamity in its tracks.

He started off with very small experiments to prove his theory, because he was cautious and he didn't know what the cosmic side effects of stopping time might be.

He prevented a bee from stinging his pet golden retriever on the nose by freezing time for three-tenths of a second and flicking the insect into a nearby rose-bush.

He stood outside his local elementary school and saved a second grader from running into traffic. Which only took two seconds.

He felt very encouraged until it occurred to him that if his invention ever fell into the hands of an unscrupulous person, it could be used for evil. Undetectable cheating at sports. Unsolvable bank *robberies. Or worse, nations might use it to attack one another clandestinely.*

So he kept his invention secret, telling only a few family members, a friendly museum director, and the president of the United States, with whom he was personally acquainted. In those days, the president liked to stay in touch with his country's geniuses at all times, and had given Hector his personal phone number.

Meanwhile, Hector carried his watch in his pocket, still testing it in small, unspectacular ways. He rescued a kitten from a trolley track. He snatched a lost balloon before it floated too high. The snippets of frozen time hardly seemed to add up at all, and since he did nothing but good deeds, he felt his work was ultimately for the best.

Until the afternoon when Hector Smiley spotted a pterodactyl perched in a tree outside his laboratory. At that moment, he knew his experiment was a failure. He knew the pterodactyl didn't belong in his era. He knew that an unlikely but entirely plausible side effect had occurred: his experiments had knocked time out of joint and allowed the creature to appear in a time where it shouldn't. He watched the pterodactyl until it leaped off the branch and soared away above the trees. Then he picked up the telephone and called President Roosevelt and admitted that his grand idea, as it turned out, contained a very serious flaw.

President Roosevelt summoned Hector Smiley to the White House to hear more about what had happened. Hector Smiley explained that by stopping time to perform his experiments, he'd disrupted the structure of the universe, sending a pterodactyl winging into a time and place it didn't belong.

The watch worked; it stopped time. But at too great a cost.

President Roosevelt thanked Hector Smiley for his efforts, and he ordered Hector to secure the watch in an obscure, untraceable, and utterly safe location, for even though its ability to freeze time might have been a huge benefit to the human race, the danger of using it far outweighed the advantages. The location Hector Smiley chose was the Veeder-Klamm Thimble and Handheld Timepiece Museum.

The Twelve-Year-Old
Who Struck Out Babe Ruth

"I don't suppose anybody knows how Hector Smiley fixed the disruptions his watch caused," said Oscar when the story was done.

"Sadly, his techniques are lost to history," confirmed Mr. Veeder.

"So I'll have to figure that part out on my own," said Oscar to himself. "Do you know anything else about the watch, Mr. Veeder?" he pressed.

"Just a little," Mr. Veeder said as he retrieved a lockbox from the bottom drawer of a display cabinet. "I have the packing material it came in. The thief left that behind."

From the lockbox, Mr. Veeder extracted a sealed plastic

freezer bag. Inside the bag was a crumbling crayon box. "This is the box it was stored in," he said. *Humdinger School Crayons* read the label. *Eight colors. Apex of Quality.* From the box, he extracted a handful of crumpled newspaper, brittle and yellow. "And this is the paper it was wrapped in."

Gently, Oscar took it. The folds and creases left over from when it had swaddled the watch were now soft, fibrous, faded, and in a few places torn.

The *Mt. Etna Evening Eagle*, it read. *April 11, 1935.* There were stories in the paper about the dustbowl in Oklahoma and about a shark somebody had caught in Florida. There was one about the fire department rescuing a cat from a tree. And then a tattered column proclaimed: *Local Sixth Grader Strikes out Babe Ruth!*

This article about baseball grabbed Oscar's attention. He scanned what was left of the text:

> *As the barnstorming Boston Braves completed their preseason tour with a game against the minor league Mt. Etna Mountaineers, Mr. George Herman Ruth, the Bambino, the Sultan of Swat, the Babe, received one of the biggest surprises of his career when Mt. Etna's favorite pitcher, twelve-year-old*

Here, a swatch of mailing tape obscured the rest of story. Oscar stuck his fingernail underneath to peel it back. The paper began to rip.

"Believe me," said Mr. Veeder, "the museum staff has tried everything. It won't come off. Since the rest of the story is hidden under there, there's nothing anybody can do."

"But—" said Oscar.

"However," continued Mr. Veeder, "if you look at the bottom, you can read the last half of the last sentence."

after the strikeout, never pitched again.

"Interesting," said Oscar. "I guess."

"As a museum curator, I think every single detail connected to every object in my collection is extremely interesting!" said Mr. Veeder.

"What do you think it means, then?" asked Oscar.

"I think it means Hector Smiley must have been in Mt. Etna around the time that game was played," said Mr. Veeder. "Otherwise, how would he have gotten the local newspaper?"

"What was he doing in Mt. Etna?" wondered Oscar.

"Dropping off the watch at the museum, is my guess," said Mr. Veeder.

"But we already knew that watch got dropped off at the museum. So this doesn't really get us anywhere, does it?" mused Oscar.

"You'd have to ask someone who's been around longer than I have," said Mr. Veeder.

"Thank you, Mr. Veeder," said Oscar.

Oscar hopped onto his bike. He knew just the person to ask. The person who had gotten him into this mess to begin with.

Little Big Man

O scar pedaled back to his neighborhood as fast as he could. After what Mr. Veeder had told him about Hector Smiley, Oscar had more questions than ever. And he figured the one person who could help him was the person who'd been in the middle of this mess since the beginning: Miss Ellington. Why had she given him a watch so powerful that President Roosevelt had ordered it locked up? How had she ended up with it in the first place? Had she seen who took it from safekeeping in the museum while she was pedaling by on her tricycle?

Had *she* taken it?

But just as he turned onto his street, Oscar saw a gleaming, white sports car parked in his driveway. For a second, he considered rocketing past. Maybe the driver wouldn't notice. But as he got closer, he realized it was too late. His dad had spotted him; he honked his horn and waved.

And as badly as Oscar wanted to talk to Miss Ellington, he pulled into his own driveway. He almost never got to talk to his father.

Oscar went up to his dad's open car window, and he saw that his father's girlfriend, Gina, also sat in the car.

"Sorry I missed your game last night, kid!" cried Oscar's dad. "But I have a project going. It's big. Huge. And important. It's huge, and it's important! I had to talk to my guys in Asia."

"Sounds like a fantastic project, Dad," Oscar said. Even though his father had moved out, and they didn't see each other very often, they were still alike in a certain way. They both got enthusiastic about things. But lately, Oscar was finding it harder and harder to get excited about his dad's projects. Since they meant he wasn't around for Oscar and his mom anymore.

"I'll tell you all about it when I finish," said his father a bit more quietly. "How was your game?"

"Oscar hit a home run," called Gina. "I saw the video. Congratulations, Oscar!"

"Thanks, Gina," murmured Oscar.

"You're kidding!" cried his father.

"Oscar for the win!" Gina added. "Look. It's right here! Some of it's a little choppy, but you can see it," Gina waved her cell phone at them.

"A home run! To clinch the game!" exclaimed his father. "How in the Hank Aaron did you manage that? I mean, I played baseball for twelve years and I never hit even one homer! Good going, Little Big Man."

Little Big Man used to be his nickname for Oscar, when Oscar was five. And at that moment, Oscar's dad grinned wider than he'd grinned since Oscar was five. "Outstanding." He reached out of the car and tousled Oscar's hair. "You're turning out great!"

"Thanks, Dad," said Oscar. "Maybe you can . . . come tonight? We're in the playoffs. We're playing the Yankees. It's a three-game series, with two games left."

"Well," said his dad, "if there are two games left, I'm sure I'll catch at least one." Just then, his cell phone rang, and he fished it out of his pocket. "Be with you in about nineteen seconds," he said to whoever was on the other end. To Oscar, he said, "Gotta go. Keep up the good work, Slugger." He started the car. Then he seemed to remember something, and shut the car off again. "By the way, I stopped by because I wanted to tell you I've been a little short on cash. Yesterday I placed a bet on a sure thing at the racetrack to make up the difference, but darned if my sure thing didn't lose by nineteen seconds and cost me my whole bankroll. I was hoping you'd tell your mom she needs to give me a couple more weeks on the check."

"I'll tell her," Oscar replied dejectedly. "Or—come to the game tonight, Dad, and you can tell Mom yourself."

"Ah," said his father, doing his best to look regretful. "See. The thing is, I have a Skype with my team in the Philippines at eight p.m. So I have to miss your game. Sorry."

"Hey! I have a new friend from the Philippines!" persisted Oscar brightly. "Her name is Lourdes! You could meet her. She—"

"That's great, Oscar," said his dad. "But you see, the people I'm talking to are twelve time zones away. When it's eight a.m. there, it's eight p.m. here, and I need to talk to them first thing in the morning. Their morning. So I have to miss your game."

Oscar tried not to show his disappointment.

In the car, Gina stared hard at her fingernails.

His dad's phone rang again. He snatched it out of his pocket again and frowned at the screen. "I really have to go, Oscar," he said. "I'll come to the next game, I promise.

Don't forget to tell your mom what I said. See ya."

"Bye, Dad," said Oscar as the car rolled down the driveway.

If he hadn't been so busy trying to save the universe, Oscar might've felt a lot sadder as he waved good-bye. But Oscar knew there might not be any more ball games for his dad to miss if he didn't accomplish his three tasks soon.

As soon as his dad and Gina were gone, he sprinted across the yard to Miss Ellington's house and pounded on her front door with all his might. And pounded. And pounded. Frustration and panic welled up in Oscar's chest. Then slowly the door opened to reveal all four feet, eight inches of Eleanor Ethel Ellington, squinting up at him.

"Why," Oscar cried, "did you give me a watch with the power to break the universe?"

"Heavens to Betsy," said Miss Ellington, her hand fluttering at her throat. "Did I do that?"

There Must Be Some Mistake

"**M**iss Ellington," said Oscar, "the watch you gave me is so powerful, it's supposed to be stored in a tamperproof, fireproof, bombproof vault in the Veeder-Klamm Museum. It's not supposed to be handed to your neighbor as a gift for watering tomatoes!"

"Oscar, what are you talking about?" asked Miss Ellington.

"The watch you gave me yesterday," Oscar said. "It's wanted by the FBI, the CIA, the Smithsonian, and NASA. Not to mention by two guys in black knocking on doors all over town."

"There must be some mistake," insisted Miss Ellington, "because the watch I gave you was a simple pocket watch. It belonged to my late husband, Mr. J. J. Ellington.

He wore it in his vest. I found it when I was cleaning out his sock drawer."

"No," said Oscar, "the watch you gave me had the ability to stop time."

"You're being ridiculous, Oscar," said Miss Ellington.

"I know," said Oscar. "But everything I'm saying is true."

"I've had enough of this conversation. You can't just come over here, knock on my door, and accuse me of giving away powerful watches!" declared Miss Ellington. She glanced at her kitchen clock. "It's getting late. Shouldn't you be preparing for your game?" She crossed her arms over her chest. She wasn't answering any more questions.

Oscar glanced at the clock, too. Only forty-five minutes until warm-ups. Oscar remembered Professor Smiley telling him how important it was for the Wildcats to beat the Yankees. He clearly wasn't going to get any answers out of Miss Ellington, and he couldn't be late to the ballpark. "You're right. I guess I should be going, Miss Ellington," replied Oscar.

"Before you go," said Miss Smiley, "there's something I'd like to give you."

"Oh, no," said Oscar, backing toward the door. "You've already given me plenty."

"Sit down. Relax. And don't start babbling about a magic watch," she said. Miss Ellington opened her broom closet and pulled out a canvas bag.

"Move that mail so I can put this down," she said.

As he scooped up the mail, Oscar noticed that a letter to Sheila Flaherty lay on top, unopened and returned. For a fleeting moment, he wondered how her great-grandson was doing at second base out in Seattle, but he felt like no matter what, the kid was probably having better luck on the diamond than he was.

Miss Ellington was saying, as she pulled a baseball glove from the bag, "This is very old, and very special."

"It's beautiful," said Oscar.

"It belonged to someone I used to know," said Miss Ellington. "I thought you might want it."

"Thanks. But Coach never puts me in the game, Miss Ellington," said Oscar, gazing at the mitt, which was so gorgeous it was almost a work of art. "I don't need a new glove."

"He put you in last night, I heard," said Miss Ellington. "And I know about your home run!" She put her hand briefly on his and squeezed. "Take the mitt. It's for you."

The glove gleamed chocolate brown and somehow, insead of reeking of mothballs, smelled like a cross between a Kentucky Derby saddle and a new motorcycle jacket. When Oscar put it on, it fit like magic.

"Thank you, Miss Ellington," he said.

"If you can spare a minute more, I'll show you how to take care of it," Miss Ellington went on, pulling a clean dust rag from the bag in her broom closet and a bottle of something called neat's-foot oil from a cabinet. "Always use exactly eleven drops," she instructed. "Like this." Carefully, she let the oil drip on the rag.

She showed Oscar how to apply the lightest possible layer to the entire surface, making it smooth, even, and so thin it hardly darkened the leather. "Work it in all the way," instructed Miss Ellington.

With the rag, Oscar rubbed the oil in. Between the fingers, into the webbing, into the stitching.

"The inside of the glove, too," prompted Miss Ellington. "People forget, but it's important, because your hand sweats on the leather and dries it out from within."

"Sometimes it seems like you know more about baseball than I do," said Oscar.

"I've been around a long time," said Miss Ellington. "I've picked up a few things."

"You picked up a *lot* about baseball," observed Oscar.

She was quiet for a bit. Then she said slowly, "I used to

play baseball, Oscar."

"Really? Why didn't you ever say?" asked Oscar.

"It's not something I think about that much," Miss Ellington said sadly.

"I wish I could have seen you play!" said Oscar. "Was this your glove?"

"Yes. My grandfather gave it to me," said Miss Ellington. "He loved baseball. He showed me how to oil it so it would never wear out."

"And now you're showing me. Thank you," said Oscar.

Miss Ellington was quiet for a while, looking at the glove. "Just remember, when life confuses you, or people disappoint you—" She paused to glance out the window at his driveway next door, and Oscar knew she had watched his whole conversation with his dad. "It helps to do something simple," concluded Miss Ellington.

"Like oil a glove?" said Oscar.

"Or water the garden," said Miss Ellington.

"Or write a letter," said Oscar, "and mail it."

"Or write a letter and mail it," affirmed Miss Ellington quietly.

"Thank you, Miss Ellington," said Oscar. "Even if I never use it in a game, even if I just warm up with it and shag flies in practice and toss pitches off the backstop and catch them on my own, this glove is perfect."

"Good luck tonight," said Miss Ellington.

Oscar left feeling hopeful—he might have destroyed the universe and lost the most powerful object known to man, but his new mitt filled him with optimism.

You're Starting Tonight

O scar arrived early for the game at Mt. Etna Diamond. Before he ran onto the field to warm up, he stood outside its looming walls and briefly contemplated their old-fashioned grandeur.

Mt. Etna Diamond was the league championship park, with parapets of cement and arches of stone, like a real, old-fashioned baseball stadium. Back in the day, the minor league Mt. Etna Mountaineers used to play here, from 1934 to 1977. And though the Mountaineers were long gone, their stately stadium remained. Now the Wildcats were playing in it to earn their place in history.

The light seemed strange. Glaring and harsh. Somewhere up there, Oscar mused as he scanned the sky, a second sun was hurtling through space, closing in, soon to take its place next to the bona fide sun. And before too long, people would notice.

"Indigo!" hollered Coach Ron. "Stop lollygagging around and get on the field! Have you seen Mangubat?"

"She'll be here, Coach," said Oscar. As crazy as the day had been, Oscar knew Lourdes wouldn't let the team down.

"She'd better!" exclaimed the coach. "'Cause without her, this team's got approximately the same chance as a snowball in Guatemala!"

Oscar glanced at Bobby Farouk, who was tightening the thumb strap on his mitt. Bobby glanced back at Oscar quizzically. Neither of them had ever heard Coach Ron make such a brutally accurate assessment of the Wildcats. Usually, he just told them winning wasn't everything, and asked if everybody's shoelaces were tied.

But now he seemed really worried. "Does anybody have the child's handle?" asked the coach about Lourdes. "Can somebody Snapchat her mom?"

"Nobody knows how to get in touch with Lourdes, Coach," said Bobby. "Nobody even knows where she lives."

And it dawned on Oscar that he actually *did* know where Lourdes lived, since he'd been in the car when she gave Mr. Llimb and Mr. Skerritt directions to her house and they'd dropped her off. Which made him the only person on the team with this knowledge. He didn't know if he should reveal it. And he really didn't know if he should volunteer to go find her, since he wasn't too sure she'd be glad to see him after the s'mores conversation.

Luckily, at that moment, he heard footsteps approaching from behind the dugout. Lourdes herself. Much improved after Mr. Llimb's miracle cure.

Lourdes saw Oscar, and her gaze went right through him as she contemplated the invisible sights that only she and a few Greek heroes and maybe Mets all-star pitcher Jacob deGrom could see. It was like Oscar wasn't there at all. Very different from a few hours ago, Oscar reflected. He'd really blown it.

And then, as if to drive that thought home, a flock of Carolina parakeets swarmed across the diamond. Oscar eyed them apprehensively. These birds, he'd learned in science class, had been extinct in the wild for over one hundred years. He counted to nineteen seconds. They promptly disappeared. This was bad.

Once the parakeets were out of sight, Oscar turned to Lourdes. He wanted to speak, but he didn't know what to say. And he wasn't sure if it was all that helpful when Vern and Suzy began voicing their opinions in his mind:

The thing is, Suzy, the window inside which you apologize to a new acquaintance isn't very big.

And it closes fast, Vern. Young Indigo had better say something quick.

Oscar glanced around. They sounded like they were sitting in their broadcast booth two feet away. But of course they weren't. Their voices emanated from his imagination. And were kind of distracting.

Already, Oscar has let the silence between himself and his teammate become painfully awkward, Suzy.

Whoever decides to start talking first is going to have to pretend like everything is fine and jump right in, Vern.

Oscar took a deep breath and psyched himself up for maximum inspiration. What if he started by apologizing?

"Sorry about your toe."

No. Didn't sound quite right. Besides, he'd already apologized for it once.

"Sorry about the ex-gangsters who took us for a ride."

Nope. After all, she'd had fun with Mr. Llimb and Mr. Skerritt. They weren't the problem. The problem was Oscar.

"Lourdes, by the way: I cheated. My home run was fake and of possibly cosmic proportions that could, according to Professor T. Buffington Smiley, lead to the shriveling of our current universe? Sorry I didn't tell you earlier?"

Uh-uh.

Perhaps it'd be good to start with something simpler: "How are you?"

Sure. He'd ask, and hopefully, Lourdes would answer. And things would progress from there. But as Oscar finally spoke, so did Lourdes, and Oscar said, "How are—" and she said, "Who will—" and he said, "Go ahead!" and she said, "No, you!" and by then, Oscar had forgotten what he wanted to say.

"Mangubat!" shouted Coach Ron. "Ready to play?"

Lourdes turned away from Oscar to nod at Coach Ron.

"Great. Listen up, Wildcats. We win this one, we take home the trophy. So let's beat those Yankees and show them who's boss! Since Lourdes pitched last night, Kevin's on the mound. Lourdes, you're on second," continued the coach. "How's the toe?"

Lourdes gave him a thumbs-up.

"Got in some physical therapy?" asked the coach. "Good!"

Oscar guessed having Mr. Llimb yank on your baby toe while Mr. Skerritt held you counted as physical therapy.

Ron listed the rest of the line-up and field assignments

until—"Oscar," said Coach Ron, "you're starting tonight in right field."

"What?" cried Oscar, not believing his ears.

"Get your glove on. Hope it's oiled up."

"It is, Coach!" cried Oscar. "It is!" He slipped on the perfect old glove Miss Ellington had given him, silently told her thanks, and pulled his hat on tight.

Despite the problems with missing watches, failed friendships, second suns, not to mention the disintegration of the universe—all of which was his fault—Oscar couldn't help it. His spirits soared. He'd been waiting his whole life to hear these words from a coach.

You're.

Starting.

Tonight.

"'Cause you hit that homer," elaborated Coach Ron.

Oscar's spirits dropped. Because he *hadn't* hit that homer. Everything came back to this.

You Haven't Heard the Last of This

Since this was game two of the series, the Yankees were the home team at Mt. Etna Diamond. Which meant the Wildcats came to bat first. Their pitcher, Robocop Roberts, who was not bad, sat Axel, Bobby, and Steve down in order.

And just like that, the bottom of the first rolled around, and the Wildcats took the field.

Oscar settled into right. Lourdes lined up in front of him at second base. She didn't look his way, and she didn't give him a big smile, or any of the stuff ace players do in stories when a rookie hits the field for the first time. But they were on the same team, playing on the same grass, and they were comrades—even if she wouldn't look at him. Even if he'd destroyed the universe.

In center stood Carlissimo Fong, popping his fist into

his glove and inspecting the turf around him for obstructions and gopher holes, just in case. And over in left, Kamran Singh glided into position like a gazelle skimming across the savannah. Until he got his feet tangled, and stumbled, and came within a centimeter of face-planting in the turf. But he regained his balance and slid to a halt, bouncing on his toes, ready for action.

Sure. Oscar was nervous. But he was in the lineup! He knew that, for the first time in his life, he belonged.

The turf was his, all his, the right half of Mt. Etna Diamond, to protect and defend. Every blade of grass, every crumb of dirt, every moth fluttering amid the final rays of the setting sun, every molecule of air.

And sure, the fate of the universe hung in the balance, but now Oscar was on the field, and he knew he'd play a part in the Wildcats' victory over the Yankees. Or at least he really, really hoped he would.

The Yanks' third baseman led off: Christopher Connolly. The Wildcats' pitcher, Kevin Truax, wound up and tossed his best fastball straight down the middle, but Chris kept his eye on the pitch and smoothly sliced it over Lourdes's head to center field for a single. And then the ball bounced into the seething vines that grew on the outfield fence, which grabbed it and wouldn't let go until

Kamran and Carlissimo both reached in, found the ball, and tore it loose, and by then Chris was on second with a ground rule double.

This must've rattled the pitcher's cage a bit, because he then gave up a single to Robocop.

And so Kevin found himself facing Taser Tompkins, the second-best hitter in the state after Lourdes Mangubat.

Unfortunately, Kevin served up a fat, juicy strike.

Taser smoked it like a meteorite over Oscar's head. It seemed to make a sizzling sound as it passed. Oscar didn't even have time to react before the ball ricocheted off the wall straight to Carlissimo, who'd run over to back him up. Carlissimo threw it home before any runners scored. But still. Three batters. Three runners on base. Not a great way to kick off the most important game the Wildcats had ever played.

And then Bif Stroganoff strolled to the plate, swinging his shiny red aluminum bat with menace.

"You got this, Kevin!" called Oscar.

Kevin wound up and threw—a curveball.

The problem with Kevin's curves was that they didn't really curve. They floated toward the plate like big, juicy beach balls, ripe to be whacked.

And at the plate stood Bif, wielding a bat large enough to stop a charging Volkswagen.

So Oscar did what he was best at. He hoped. He hoped the curveball would actually curve. He hoped Bif would whiff. Or, if not, he hoped Bif would fall down, or a bug would land in his eye. He hoped that something, anything, would keep him from belting a grand slam in the very first inning of the game, the game upon which the future of the universe, thanks to Oscar, depended.

Bif swung. And smacked the living tar out of poor Kevin's sad alleged curveball.

A maelstrom whirled in Oscar's brain. Hope and fear. Optimism and dread. The colors of the night ran together. Edges blurred and sounds muddled. Bif's shot flew straight at Oscar, and Oscar jabbed his glove in the air. He hoped for the best. And then by some miracle, the ball smacked right into the soft, supple pocket of his baseball mitt. He'd caught it! Bif was out! But as Oscar jubilated, the Yankee on third tagged up and started running toward home.

Oscar drew back and hurled the ball toward the catcher. His throw arrived half an inch ahead of the runner. "Yer out!" cried the ump as Axel nabbed him.

Axel then zipped the ball to third, and Layton Brooks

caught it neatly, tagging out the oncoming runner. Three outs. End of the inning.

"Awesome, Oscar!" he heard Kevin Truax cry. "You started a triple play! You saved a run!"

"Wow" was all Coach Ron had to say as Oscar trotted to the dugout.

And Oscar felt like part of everything that had ever gone right on a baseball diamond in the entire history of the game.

It was all he had dreamed of, and more. He scanned the stands. No sign of his mom. And his dad hadn't made it. But what was that voice, high and strong above all the others, cheering: "Way to wing it, Oscar!"? Miss Ellington! At his game! Oscar couldn't help it. He grinned from ear to ear and pumped his fist in the air. Miss Ellington pumped her translucent, delicate, liver-spotted fist right back. She'd known he needed somebody there to cheer for him. She'd come.

Mr. Skerritt and Mr. Llimb tipped their hats from high in the third-base stands. Oscar sent a dab their way. He realized he was starting to like those guys.

And he knew he'd tell his mom about the triple play after she got home from work. And he'd tell his dad, too, next time they talked. He'd done something great at the game and hadn't even cheated! Surely this was a good sign—a step in the right direction.

"Nice play," said Lourdes, dropping onto the bench beside him.

"Thanks," said Oscar.

And that was how Oscar Indigo solved the problem of what to say to Lourdes Mangubat. When all else fails, talk about baseball, even if you only exchange three words. At least it's a start.

Silence descended between them. Oscar stared at his mitt. Then he noticed a set of letters, possibly initials, carved into his glove: EES. Huh. Miss Ellington's, from when she was young? He wondered idly to himself what Eleanor Ethel Ellington's last name used to be. Something beginning with *S*.

When he looked up, the Yankees were taking the field for the top of the second inning. Taser stomped out to the mound to pitch.

When Coach Ron saw Taser, though, he went charging from the dugout. "That's against the rules! He pitched last night! He's not allowed back on the mound for two days! You're just putting him in because he's your best pitcher!"

The umpire, who was Bobby's granddad Mr. Farouk again, squinted at Taser. "It seems to me that he did pitch yesterday," said Mr. Farouk.

"What?" cried Coach Pringle, sprinting out of the Yankees' dugout. "That's nuts! This kid didn't pitch yesterday!"

"Did you pitch yesterday?" Mr. Farouk asked Taser.

"No way," said Taser, staring at him like he'd lost his mind. "What are you talking about?"

"What's the problem?" asked Taser's mom, huffing and puffing her way into the middle of the small crowd on the mound.

"Nothing, Mrs. Tompkins," said Mr. Farouk. "I have this under control. Please return to the stands."

"As the president of the Slugger League board of directors," declared Taser's mom, "I have a right to know what the problem is."

"You *know* what it is," shot back Coach Ron. "Your coach is trying to pitch your son two games in a row."

"Prove it," said Sheila Tompkins.

"Yeah," said Taser. "Prove it."

"Wait," said Mr. Farouk, digging around in the pocket of his giant black umpire jacket. "I still have last night's lineup card."

Sheila Tompkins and Coach Pringle exchanged uneasy looks.

"Deli pickup number," said Mr. Farouk, sorting through a stack of rumpled paper. "Comcast bill. Car wash code. Here it is!" He held a battered card six inches from his nose and squinted. He began to read aloud. "Wildcats vs. Yankees, July 5: Pitching for the Yank—"

"Let me see that!" shrieked Taser's mom. She snatched it from Mr. Farouk. She looked it over. A rogue gust of wind blasted in from left field. Somehow, the card slipped away from her and fluttered away over the bleachers. "Whoops!" cried Mrs. Tompkins.

"I do not think—" began Mr. Farouk. But the noise and the dust of the wind gust made it impossible to communicate.

And this lasted for almost exactly nineteen seconds, Oscar couldn't help noticing.

"With no proof," shouted Mr. Farouk over the dying wind, ruefully gazing in the direction the lineup card had disappeared, "I have no choice but to allow the young man to pitch."

"That's not fair!" cried Coach Ron.

"Since I have no evidence, my hands are tied," said Mr. Farouk.

"I'll file a protest!" said Coach Ron, though he clearly realized that protests were futile.

"You should. Maybe you'll win. I would love to be overruled," said Mr. Farouk. "But Taser's mother is the president of the league board of directors. I think your chances are slim. Now. Play ball!"

And play ball they did. And surprisingly, despite the Yankees' pitching shenanigans, the Wildcats had some luck of their own. Lourdes smacked a homer off Taser.

And even though Taser threw his glove in the dirt, Coach Pringle was heard to shout, "It's OK! Nothing but a lucky shot! She's no good! She's just a girl! We'll score ten runs when we come up to bat!"

As Lourdes passed third, Robocop stuck his foot out to trip her, but pretending not to notice, she scampered home to put the Wildcats ahead.

Wildcats 1, Yankees 0.

And after that, the Wildcats held their lead for the next six innings. Coach Ron was ecstatic, but no one was happier than Oscar. He felt like he was getting somewhere.

The universe, unfortunately, seemed to have other plans.

By the eighth inning, Kevin's arm had gotten so tired he could barely get the ball to the plate. He let Robocop on base with a walk. Then Taser came to bat and watched two of Kevin's weakening pitches go by, and grinned and waggled his bat, knowing Kevin's arm had turned to Jell-O. After that, Taser knocked the next pitch out of the park, driving in Robocop, not to mention himself. He took off around the bases at a leisurely pace, gloating all the way home.

Yanks 2. Wildcats 1.

The top of the ninth rolled around.

It was the final at-bat for the Wildcats. Coach Ron looked nervous.

"Wildcats," he said in the dugout, "this is it. We've got half an inning to put ourselves in the lead. Three outs. Nine strikes. We *need* this win. Who's up?" He checked his roster. "Mangubat? Go out there and knock it a mile!"

Lourdes did her best, but all she could manage was a single.

Carlissimo Fong struck out on three straight pitches.

Layton Brooks suffered Carlissimo's fate, too.

And then . . . it was time. Coach Ron checked the lineup sheet. The entire team held its breath as it waited to hear who was up next, although everybody already knew. "Oscar?" Coach Ron's voice wavered.

Oscar swallowed. Here he was again. The game resting

on his shoulders, and this time, along with it, the universe.

"We could use another homer," said the coach encouragingly. "We need somebody to drive in two runs. Go out there and bring in Mangubat, and while you're at it, bring yourself around, too."

Ice formed along Oscar's spine. His lungs hardened into stone. His legs refused to move.

"Listen, son," said the coach. "Whatever your mojo is, you need to unleash it again. Right now."

"I don't know if I can unleash my mojo today," said Oscar.

"Why not?" asked the coach.

"I left it in the bread box," said Oscar.

"What?" asked Coach Ron.

"I mean, I don't think I have my mojo with me right now," said Oscar.

"If you had it with you last night, then you have it with you tonight," Coach Ron reassured him. "People don't lose their mojo that fast."

"Maybe some people do," said Oscar. "People like me."

"Listen, Oscar," said the coach. "We appreciate the high fives and the enthusiastic grins you've displayed all these years. We really do. We like the OscarAde. Pretty much. But high fives and ear-to-ear smiles and OscarAde don't win baseball games. Home runs win baseball games. And I'd really like to win this baseball game."

"I would, too, Coach," said Oscar. He missed the old Coach Ron. The nice one. The one who told them things were OK no matter what. But he knew that coach was now going the way of the bees. One more wrong for Oscar to put right.

"Then go out there and smack the ball over the fence just like you did last night!" shouted Coach Ron.

"Right," gulped Oscar. "Like I did last night."

"Batter up!" called the umpire.

Oscar made his way to the plate. It was only ten yards from the dugout, but it took him over a hundred and fifty years to get there. Or at least that's how much he felt like he'd aged during the journey. The crowd had gone silent.

Oscar thought of Lourdes, out there on base, depending on him to get her home. Mr. Llimb and Mr. Skerritt were watching, along with Miss Ellington and half of East Mt. Etna. He stepped up to the plate.

The light of the setting sun seemed strange, and far stronger than usual. For now, Oscar was the only one who knew why: a second sun, intensifying the light of the first.

Taser drew back. He fired straight at Oscar's ribcage.

Oscar danced out of the way. Just in time. The ball whomped off the backstop.

Ball one. Wild pitch. Taser didn't care. So what if he was now one pitch behind in the count? So what if Lourdes had trotted to second base? It was worth burning a toss, giving up a ball, letting the runner advance, just to show Oscar who was boss.

Now he was going to throw three straight strikes and send Oscar and the rest of the Wildcats home with tears in their little loser eyes.

Taser wound up. He launched a rocket. Steeeerike one.

Indigo has been here before, Vern.

And remember, he delivered a fat, juicy home run, Suzy.

All he needs is one good pitch, Vern.

Taser served up the next toss. The ball came at Oscar like a torpedo zooming down a pipe. Except harder to see. Steeeerike two.

Prospects are looking a little dimmer for Oscar Indigo, Suzy.

The kid is doing his best, Vern. Let's hope it's going to be good enough.

Taser came set on the mound. He went into his motion.

Oscar gripped the bat. He locked onto the ball. The

lights blazed. The base paths rolled like ocean waves. Panic rose like a tide in his gullet. The pitch seemed to be headed for his ear.

He ducked.

He heard the plink of leather against aluminum. Felt the sting of the bat on his fingers.

He opened his eyes. The ball rolled slowly away from him in front of the plate.

"Fair ball!" called the umpire.

"Run, Oscar! Run!" voices yelled from the Wildcats' dugout.

"What—" Oscar cried. But he realized in a flash what'd happened. Taser had been trying to pitch close to his head. And when he ducked, his bat poked straight up in the air behind him. Accidentally, he'd hit the ball. At least seven whole feet.

So he started running.

Lourdes was already halfway to third.

Oscar sprinted for first.

The Yankees catcher Bif Stroganoff scrambled to pick up the ball and hurl it toward first.

Oscar closed in on the bag. He galloped like he'd just robbed a bank. By the look in the first baseman's eyes, Oscar could tell that Bif was about to make the throw.

Would he get to first base in time? Oscar gave it more gas. He stretched his stride out and pumped his arms and ignored the burning in his thighs.

His foot hit the base.

The ball hit the first baseman's glove.

"Safe!" he heard the ump yell.

But as he crossed the bag, he could tell the play wasn't over. A chorus of cheers exploded from the bleachers.

"Home! Home! Home!" cried the Yankees infield.

Oscar saw Lourdes rounding third and pushing for home.

Oscar could only watch helplessly as the Yankees' first baseman fired to Bif Stroganoff, who was guarding home plate. Lourdes dove, but she was too late. Bif blocked her way like a midsize dump truck, clutching the ball in his mitt.

The ump cried, "Yer out!"

A stunned silence fell. Lourdes climbed to her knees but couldn't seem to stand. A look of horror crossed her face. She'd just made the biggest error of the series—of the season—and the Yankees had won the game.

Suzy and Vern let their opinions be known.

Young Indigo did his best, Vern.

Mangubat just got too ambitious, Suzy.

There's where you're right, Vern. Sometimes, the tale doesn't end "happily ever after."

Of course, the Yankees flooded the field, and Yankee jubilation ruled.

Wise people say: *There's nothing worse than a sore loser.*

Wiser people add: *except a sore winner.*

The Yankees were not wise people.

"Lourdes, did you bring your lunch money?" cried Taser, dancing around the infield.

"'Cause we just took you to school!" added Robocop. "Bwaahaahaahaahaa!"

"Do the Robot, boys!" cried Taser's mother.

Which was the cue for Taser and Robocop to demonstrate how Robocop had earned his nickname. Taser pretended to turn a giant key on Robocop's back. Once he'd wound Robo up all the way, Robocop transformed into an automated fist-bumping machine. A life-size Rock'em Sock'em Robot. He bumped all the Yankees players once, twice, three times.

Then he roboted himself over to the Wildcats' dugout and began bumping fists with them. Which was not a whole lot of fun for the Wildcats, since if they ignored him, they seemed like bad sports, and if they bumped him back, he laughed.

People say Robocop Roberts thought that routine up himself, Suzy.

When he was five, Vern.

It never gets old, Suzy.

Well, it kind of does, Vern.

When Robocop got to Lourdes, she tried to ignore him, but he scooted himself in front of her no matter which way she turned. "Lourdes," he said in a flat, robot voice, "you played a very nice game. For a girl." And even though his voice was machinelike, his eyes shone with malice. He turned and bumped Taser, who was standing beside him.

Lourdes trembled with anger.

"Why are you mad?" demanded Taser, watching her closely. "He was being nice!"

"Shut up!" cried Lourdes.

"You did your best," said Taser. "The problem is, you rot. So your best wasn't good enough!"

"Leave her alone!" Oscar cried, stepping in between the bullies and Lourdes.

"Who's gonna make us?" sneered Taser.

"You?" jeered Robocop. "Ha!"

"How about if *I* make you stop?" came a voice from behind Oscar.

"Let me know if you need help," chimed in a second. Mr. Llimb and Mr. Skerritt.

Taser glanced up and saw the two men. He tried not to look scared, but Oscar saw the color leave his face.

"Whatever. I'm out of here. See you losers next game," said Taser, backing away. He scuttled after Robocop, who was already halfway across the parking lot. Clearly, Robocop remembered their last meeting.

"Lourdes," called Oscar, but she was already stalking toward the gate, head down. "It's OK to make a mistake once in a while," he told her.

She stiffened and turned back to face him.

"It's not OK! I lost the game!" snapped Lourdes. "People are making fun of me! I'm a complete failure."

"But it's just one game—" said Oscar. He did his best to sound upbeat.

"Stop being so positive all the time!" yelled Lourdes. "It's exasperating!"

She crossed the street to the bus stop just as the bus pulled up. When it roared away, she was gone.

In the silence, Oscar said to Mr. Llimb and Mr.

Skerritt, "She's right. I shouldn't be so positive. I haven't found the watch. I have no idea how to put the nineteen seconds back, and we didn't beat the Yankees. And now Lourdes is mad at me."

"Professor Smiley told us to tell you that all adds up to a huge problem," said Mr. Llimb. "But he said if we're lucky, things may hold together until tomorrow's game. And if they do, you have one last chance to win."

"Plus we've got one more thing to tell you," added Mr. Skerritt. "Something's going on in the Mt. Etna stadium. There's this fellow wearing an old-fashioned Boston Braves uniform. I would think he's another one of those nineteen-second flibbertigibbets, but he's been sticking around a lot longer than that."

"Really?" asked Oscar. "Where is he?"

"Just kind of hovering by himself at the end of the bleacher seats," said Mr. Llimb. "Like a ghost."

"I'm going to talk to him," said Oscar. "Even if he's a ghost. I want to see why Boston Braves are shadowing me and find out what he knows." He shivered slightly.

"You need our help?" asked Mr. Llimb.

"No, thanks," said Oscar. "I've got this. But I appreciate the offer."

The Mt. Etna Mountaineers

As he climbed the deserted stadium steps under the eerie light of the second sun, fully visible now that the first had set, Oscar shuddered. He didn't feel any braver about ghosts than the next guy, but he had to save the universe, so acting like a fraidycat was not a luxury he could afford.

Besides, up close, this ghost didn't seem all that scary. He seemed more like a gum-chewing shortstop than an unquiet spirit.

"Hello?" Oscar asked tentatively as he sat down in the top row of the bleachers. "Can you hear me?"

"Of course," said the ballplayer, who, upon closer inspection, appeared to be chewing tobacco, not gum. "But ain't you afraid of ghosts?"

"A little," admitted Oscar. "I probably wouldn't be talking to you if I didn't need to ask you something really badly."

"Shoot," said the old Brave.

Somehow Oscar's mind went blank. What do you ask a specter? Then a question popped into his mind, one that must've been floating around in there since he'd visited the Veeder-Klamm Museum.

"Did a kid ever strike out Babe Ruth? In this ballpark? A twelve-year-old? When he played for the Boston Braves?" asked Oscar. "I'm only asking because you're a Boston Brave, so maybe you know?"

"Funny you should mention that," said the player, eyeing Oscar closely. "I played in that game. I'll tell you what I remember. And by the way, my name is Pinky Whitney."

"I'm Oscar Indigo," said Oscar. "Pleased to meet you, Mr. Whitney." Oscar grinned. He couldn't help it. Braving a conversation with this Brave had turned out to be the right thing to do.

"We were barnstorming," said Pinky Whitney. "You know, playing preseason games in small towns and out-of-the-way cities against local teams for publicity, and to make a few extra bucks. . . ."

The Story of *The Drop*,
as told by Pinky Whitney

April 11, 1935

By the time the game started, there were five thousand spectators in the stands. Word spread fast. The Babe stepped to the plate, and a few people cheered for him, but most of those five thousand fans were cheering for the Mountaineers' pitcher. See, this game and this town were special. They had a twelve-year-old phenom named E. E. Smiley.

Babe didn't know it, but Smiley had a special pitch. It had its own nickname: The Drop.

People said the Mountaineers' manager, a son-of-a-gun named Razor Tompkins, had only signed the sixth grader to pitch as a publicity stunt. But no one told this to E. E. Smiley. And that The Drop wasn't any publicity stunt. It was the real deal.

So, the Babe's at bat. Smiley winds up and delivers the first pitch. It sails over the plate for a strike.

The Babe shrugs like that isn't a big deal and gets ready for the next pitch.

E. E. Smiley winds up again like a coffee grinder and lets The Drop fly. And drop it does. Down below

Babe Ruth's knees. The Sultan of Swat takes a staggering cut. But he misses.

Strike two.

The hometown crowd is going wild at this point. Smiley's giving old Babe a run for his money. And Smiley's only twelve!

Babe Ruth shrugs. And he smiles a little. But not much—he's shaken up!

So E. E. Smiley lobs what looks like an easy floater. The pitch dances through the air on butterfly wings. The Babe's eyes zero in on it. But he never moves. He seems frozen by the deceptiveness of that pitch. And the ball sails over the plate and into the catcher's mitt.

"Steeeeee-rike three! Yer out!"

The Babe struck out looking. Very strange. You don't see that every day.

As I remember, he said something to the pitcher, which made her look real upset. Then Ruth broke his bat over his knee, threw the pieces on the ground, and stalked to his dugout. Hard to hear what he said over the hometown cheering, though.

E. E. Smiley pitched the rest of the inning, notching a fly out and another strikeout. But she didn't come out of the dugout for the second inning, and she never played another game for the Mountaineers as far as I know. Or for any other team. I always figured I'd hear about her later, but she disappeared from baseball history.

And Babe Ruth retired two months later.

"Wait," said Oscar when Whitney had finished. "E. E. Smiley was a sixth-grade *girl?*"

"Didn't I mention that?" asked Pinky.

"No," said Oscar.

"Don't know if it matters or not, 'cause she struck out the Bambino, and that's what counts, right?"

But while Pinky Whitney was answering, Oscar remembered the initials EES inscribed on Miss Ellington's mitt. "Mr. Whitney?" asked Oscar. "Do you know what 'E. E.' stood for?"

But Pinky Whitney had faded away, leaving Oscar alone in the empty stadium.

"That's OK," said Oscar into the silence. "I'll put it on the list of things I need to ask Miss Ellington when I see her again. Miss *Eleanor Ethel* Ellington."

Outside the ballpark gates, the Corolla came rattling around the corner. Oscar ran to meet it. Maybe it was just as well the second sun refused to set. Both of his mother's headlights appeared to be broken now.

"Is everything OK?" asked Oscar's mom when she saw him.

"Sure," said Oscar, though his mind raced with the story Pinky Whitney had just told him.

"You look like you just saw a ghost," said his mother.

"No, of course I didn't, why did you say that—oh—good one, Mom," replied Oscar, finally realizing she was joking.

"The game is over?" she asked.

"Yes. It's been over for a while now," said Oscar.

"Just my luck," said his mother. "If I had to get fired, why couldn't I get fired in time to make it to your game?"

"That is rotten luck," said Oscar. "Wait. You got fired?" The news chilled him. First, it's never good when your mom gets fired. Second, it was another of the signs T. Buffington Smiley had mentioned: *Good people will fail . . . friends and loved ones will experience disappointment and defeat.*

"Yes," said his mother. "But it wasn't a totally terrible night, because you won your game."

"Actually, we lost," said Oscar.

"Oh. A last-second score?" His mother sounded

defeated. Oscar wished he had better news.

"Something like that," said Oscar.

"That's OK, though. One game doesn't make any difference in the overall, gigantic, cosmic, grand scheme of things. Right?" said his mother.

"This one kind of did, Mom," said Oscar. "It really did." He wished he could talk to her about the mess he was in. But he couldn't, especially when she'd just lost her job. "I'm sorry you got fired."

"It was the craziest thing," she replied. "I'd just steamed the most perfect Mochalino Supremo in history, but when I turned around to pour it, the cup I'd set on the counter was gone! The Mochalino splattered all over the counter and into the lap of the lady who ordered it. Mr. Parker fired me on the spot."

"I'm sorry, Mom," said Oscar, and his stomach dropped. "How long does it take to steam a Mochalino Supremo, anyway?"

As if he didn't already know the answer.

"Nineteen seconds," said his mother.

"Why did I bother to ask?" Oscar muttered.

"What, honey?"

"Nothing," said Oscar.

"I wish it'd happened in time for me to see the end

of your game, even just to see you snatch defeat from the jaws of victory," said his mother.

"Nobody's put it that way yet," said Oscar ruefully. "Wow. Thanks."

"You're welcome. For me, it's not whether you win or lose. It's how you play the game, honey. Anyway, getting fired is the best thing that ever happened to me. I'm going to apply at Rossini's. Tomorrow. Listen. I've already got my audition tunes ready." And with that, she sang. She sang and sang. She sang "God Bless the Child." She sang "Satin Doll." She sang "Summertime." And while she sang, for a few minutes, it was summertime just like summertime was supposed to be, with fireflies and cicadas and the aroma of freshly cut grass wafting through the windows. Not ghosts and pterodactyls and Robocops and second suns. Oscar wished the ride home would never be over. He wished his mother's song would last forever.

But eventually, they rolled into the driveway and parked under the weird orange sky. And Oscar remembered what his dad had asked him to say. He didn't want to ruin the moment, but his mom had just lost one of her jobs, so he knew he'd better say it. "Dad stopped by this afternoon."

"Oh?" said his mother nonchalantly.

A good start. Her happy mood seemed to be holding up. "He said he's really busy with his project, and he has a lot going on, and he's going to be late with the check," Oscar blurted as fast as he could.

"Was Gina along for the ride?" asked his mother breezily, as if none of this information really bothered her.

"Yes. She told me congratulations on the, uh, home run," said Oscar.

"Poor girl," said his mother. "One day, I hope she'll wise up. And get over your dad. Just like I did. Because I am. Completely. Over him. I'm a winner now! Like you, Oscar! You're my hero! Rossini's, here I come!" And as she dropped her keys in her purse, she sang the last verse of "Summertime" again, for all the world to hear. And burst into tears. "I can't believe he left," she sobbed. "I don't understand."

"I'm sorry, Mom" was all Oscar could say.

Twenty minutes later, Oscar sat on his bed with Dr. Soul. Streaks of red stained the western sky. Darkness would've descended two hours before if not for the lurid new sun. His mother was still awake, sitting by herself in the living room, singing the sad song that had no words. Oscar recorded his mother's song on his phone, just for a bit, because he didn't want it to drift away into the night and be lost forever.

"I've got to fix things, Dr. Soul," said Oscar. He gazed out his window. Sleep felt farther away than Kamchatka.

The breeze sighed against Oscar's window screen like it had done every summer night he could remember, and he heard the forest leaves rustle until a rush of wind swelled the whisper into a roar, as if a green ocean had rolled nearby in the darkness.

Then everything fell silent. Peace, just a moment of it, seemed to descend.

"I can do this!" Oscar said to himself. The same overwhelming hope that had filled him at the beginning of every baseball game filled him now. "I'm going to find the watch and put the nineteen seconds back, and the Wildcats are going to beat the Yankees fair and square." He turned to his cat. "Dr. Soul, where do you think the watch is?"

Dr. Soul licked his right paw and used it to rub his ear. He didn't reply. "No offense, Dr. Soul," said Oscar, "but I really need a partner who can talk." He petted his cat silently for a moment. "I need a *friend* who can talk," he added. "I have to find Lourdes."

He listened for his mother's singing downstairs, but he couldn't hear her. She'd fallen asleep. Oscar slid his window screen open.

He stepped through his dormer window and felt with his toes for a foothold on the pebbly shingles outside.

Dr. Soul just watched with a look in his eye that said: *Even cats should be in bed right now, Oscar.* He leaped to the windowsill as Oscar stepped outside. *Have fun*, Dr. Soul seemed to say. *I'm staying home.*

Creeping along the ledge beneath his high window, Oscar let his eyes adjust to the odd, orange sky, and in the momentary calm, he located the branch of a linden tree that overhung his roof.

Stepping onto it, he made his way along the bough to the linden's trunk.

When he got to the trunk, he stepped around it to a branch growing on the far side. Down this branch, over his backyard fence, he crept into the dark canopy of the Tuscarora Woods.

From limb to limb, from tree to tree, he stole deeper into the greeny darkness. Eventually, he came to the tallest tree in Mt. Etna, a sycamore. But instead of climbing down, he climbed up.

From the very top, he took in the sight of the town lying quietly, sparkling, and momentarily safe beneath him. There was no actual East or West Mt. Etna. This was just a distinction the Yankees and their families had made up so they could feel superior. Up here, none of that mattered.

Oscar set the arches of his feet into the topmost Y of the tree, reclining against one branch of the split, observing the stars as they played peekaboo through the orangey glow of that ever-near second sun.

And something about their certainty, their age-old and up until now unchanging array, made it just plain hard to believe any of this was happening.

Maybe T. Buffington Smiley was wrong about the whole thing?

But from his great height, Oscar could still see the last particles of dusky red in the western sky, the second sun hanging on.

That brought him back to reality. To his mission. Far below, on a distant street, where a light shone in a window. The only light in the entire town of Mt. Etna, East or West. And it was coming from what Oscar now knew was Lourdes Mangubat's house.

She must be sleepless, just like him.

Exactly what Oscar had been hoping to see.

He climbed down from his tree.

"I need help," said Oscar when Lourdes opened her door.

"I thought you'd never ask," replied Lourdes. "But it might be good if you'd tell me what's going on."

"I can't. You'll think I'm terrible," said Oscar. "A horrible teammate and an awful friend."

Lourdes thought this over. "No," she finally said, stepping outside to sit on the porch, "you're a good friend, and an awesome teammate. Believe me. I know one when I see one."

"How?" Oscar murmured.

"I've been on all kinds of baseball teams, Oscar. And do you know why I finally joined the Wildcats? When I could have been on the West Mt. Etna Select Elite Pro-Development Yankees, or for that matter, the North Dallas All-Stars or the San Francisco Choice?"

"All of us Wildcats kind of wonder about that," said Oscar, sitting beside her. "Since you're so awesome, and we're not."

"I used to live in Texas," said Lourdes. "I was on TV all the time. My team won the state championship three years in a row. And I'm not bragging when I say it was because of me, mostly. That's just the truth. Any of my teammates would agree."

"Wow," said Oscar.

"But I didn't like it one bit. I was scared all the time. I had never lost a game pitching, and all I ever felt was afraid, because I knew that one day I *would* lose, and when I did, my teammates would be happy, because they hated me for being so good. My batting average was .702. And they all despised me for it. We were enemies. Everybody secretly wanted everybody else to blow it, so *they* could be the best, and we were all jealous when anybody did anything great, and the moms and dads were worse than we were. And do you know what people said to me every time I made a play?"

"I—I think I do, actually," replied Oscar. "They said you're pretty good for a girl?"

"Yes," hissed Lourdes, angry at just the thought. "It got so bad, I couldn't sleep at night. I never felt like eating. I wanted to quit. But my mom said how about if we move? And find a team that's just average? You can play for them, and nobody will care if you win or lose. Nobody will make cracks about your being a girl. You'll play just for fun, like you're supposed to. We looked all over the country, and we decided on the Wildcats, and Mom found a job in Mt. Etna, and we moved, so I could play baseball without having to hate it, without being afraid of making a mistake, or committing an error, or just plain losing every time I suited up."

"Wow. Thanks on behalf of all the Wildcats," said Oscar. "I'm glad we're so bad we don't put any pressure on you." He grinned.

"Me, too," said Lourdes, smiling back. "Still, even though you all seemed nice, I thought it would be safer not to make friends with any of you."

"We noticed," said Oscar.

"I wanted to duck the pressure," said Lourdes. "And it was fun, just showing up to play with nobody depending on me. But then the Wildcats got better."

"We all tried harder because of you. We wanted to live up to your example," replied Oscar.

"But that's the thing. Even when we starting winning, things were still OK. Because when the Wildcats got good, they turned out to be a team—a real team—what a team is supposed to be. And that's because of you, Oscar. You have more team spirit than some entire countries. That's why I wanted to be friends with you. Why I came to your house and followed you when Mr. Llimb and Mr. Skerritt were with you. But I blew it and lost the big game.

I'm sorry I was so rude to you tonight. I never blew a game before. I thought it was the worst thing that could ever happen to me. I thought you'd all hate me. I thought the universe would come to an end. But I should have known none of that would happen. The Wildcats were awesome, even though we lost. And you were the best Wildcat of all. I could never think you were a terrible teammate, or a terrible friend."

"Thanks," said Oscar. He fell silent. Maybe Lourdes *would* understand if he told her what he'd done? It would feel good to get it off his chest. So Oscar Indigo took a deep breath, gathered his courage, and said, "I know you wonder what's been going on with me. So here it is. I'm not who you think I am."

"You're not Oscar Indigo?" replied Lourdes.

"Yes. I'm Oscar Indigo. But Oscar Indigo is not who you think he is."

"Then who is Oscar Indigo?" asked Lourdes.

"He's a— *I'm* a loser!" said Oscar. "Because of something awful I did."

"I don't believe it," said Lourdes. "I mean, I believe you did *something*, because of the black Cadillac and Mr. Llimb and Mr. Skerritt, and all the whispering, but I don't believe it was awful."

"I just got so tired of losing," moaned Oscar.

"Oscar!" she replied. "You're a winner!"

"Come on, Lourdes," said Oscar. "My baseball career is one big Team Spirit plaque."

"But you've never missed a practice," Lourdes pointed out. "You've never missed a game."

"It's not that hard to get to practice, or games either," pointed out Oscar. "You can get your mom to take you, or walk, or ride your bike, or take the bus. Just about anybody can do it."

"You invented the team cheer!" said Lourdes.

"Yeah . . . *East Mt. Etna, East Mt. Etna, East Mt. Etna, wow! Ain't nobody gonna keep the Wildcats down*," said Oscar unenthusiastically. "Doesn't even rhyme."

"You mix up the OscarAde," persisted Lourdes.

"That half the team pours out the back of the dugout on the poison ivy," said Oscar.

"You holler advice at people while they're on base," said Lourdes.

"And get them thrown out," said Oscar.

"You take more practice swings and do more pushups and run more laps than anybody," said Lourdes, "and you get better all the time."

"That's not as good as it sounds," said Oscar. "At least

not for me. For you, it's great. If *you* get any better, you'll be ready for the majors. But guys like me are so far behind that even if we improve every season, we have to live to eight hundred to actually be any good."

"But you give a hundred percent every practice!" protested Lourdes.

"Sure," said Oscar. "I give one hundred percent in practice because I never get to play in *games.*"

"You do the little things right!" pointed out Lourdes.

"Because I'm horrible at anything big," said Oscar.

"What about the secret ingredient?" asked Lourdes. "In OscarAde?"

"You don't want me to tell you about the secret ingredient," warned Oscar.

"Yes I do!" said Lourdes.

"A drop of Old Spice aftershave from the bottle my dad left when he moved out," said Oscar. "To add zip."

"Eeeeeuuuw," said Lourdes.

"I told you," said Oscar.

"But you—I—" said Lourdes. "I didn't know you realized all that about yourself."

"All these years, I know everybody thought I didn't know any better, because I was just a cute little guy who wanted to play baseball. But I knew. I knew how bad I was. I'm so tired of being the supportive, enthusiastic kid who's just happy to be here," said Oscar.

"You're wrong about yourself, Oscar," said Lourdes.

"How?" Oscar asked.

"It's one thing to keep trying when you think you're going to succeed. And it's a totally different thing, and a hundred times better, to keep trying even when you know your chances are one in a thousand," she said. "Your spirits keep everyone else's up!"

"Thanks, Lourdes," said Oscar.

"It's true. I wanted you to know what I think," said Lourdes.

"But there's more to all this, Lourdes," said Oscar. "The thing is, I cheated. When I hit that home run? I didn't really hit that home run. I used a highly advanced, extremely sophisticated, incredibly dangerous scientific instrument to disrupt the flow of time so I could—well, it's kind of a long story—but the thing is, I didn't really bat that ball over the fence the other night. I fudged it."

"Wow," responded Lourdes. "I thought you just corked your bat or something simple like that."

"Lourdes, I haven't even told you the worst of it," continued Oscar. "When I did all this, I set in motion the destruction of the universe as we know it." And he told her the whole story. From the watch buried in Miss Smiley's mail to "nineteen Mississippi" to the fake home run. From Hector Smiley to the mysterious theft at the Veeder-Klamm Museum to the cosmic tomato bush to the twelve-year-old girl who struck out Babe Ruth and never pitched again. Lourdes took in every word. She didn't question a single thing, or seem surprised by any of it. As crazy as the whole story was, she seemed to believe Oscar. And when Oscar finished, she said only, "It sounds like everything leads back to Miss Ellington."

"I'm glad to hear you say that," replied Oscar, "because I've been thinking the same thing."

This Explains a Lot

In the darkness, Oscar led Lourdes to Miss Ellington's house. Both suns had set, and the night had finally grown dark. In Miss Ellington's yard, Oscar said, "Take a breath. Those are her tomato plants. Smell them?"

Lourdes breathed deep. "Delicious" was her only reply.

Dr. Soul, watching from Oscar's windowsill next door, leaped to the nearest tree limb and then to the ground.

When Oscar knocked on the back door, it swung open. He stepped inside. "Miss Ellington?" he called.

Lourdes and Dr. Soul followed behind. Oscar switched on the light.

Everything lay perfectly still, although Oscar felt like Miss Ellington might walk in at any moment to begin scolding him because he hadn't introduced his new friend. But as the seconds passed, the house only creaked emptily.

Miss Ellington was gone. And it felt like she was never coming back.

Oscar took a seat at the kitchen table, in front of the unruly pile of mail. The clutter looked exactly the same as it had when they'd oiled the glove Miss Ellington had given him earlier that day.

"Something's up with her," said Oscar. "She wrote letters to her friends every week. She had a system. She kept everything organized. Until two days ago. I don't know what happened." He lifted her address book out of the pile.

"Why do so many addresses have lines through them?" wondered Lourdes, glancing over his shoulder as he flipped through the pages.

"A lot of her friends—" began Oscar. "A lot of her friends weren't—didn't—couldn't—a lot of her friends have died. But not everybody. Look." He tabbed to *F*. "Sheila Flaherty is still—" Oscar froze before he said anything more. Because Sheila's name and address were crossed out, too.

"Oh no!" cried Oscar. As he lifted the address book to look more closely, a sheet of paper, folded into thirds, slid out and fluttered to the floor. Dr. Soul pounced on it like it was a bird. And when he realized it wasn't, he got busy licking his paws, cool as a cucumber, like nothing had ever happened.

Lourdes picked the letter up. She opened it. "It's a note to Miss Ellington," said Lourdes. "It's from—Bryan Flaherty?"

"Read it," said Oscar softly, though he already knew what it would say.

"Dear Miss Ellington," Lourdes began.

"I'm sorry to have to deliver this news, but my mother won't be answering your last letter. As you know, she has been very ill for the past year, and last night shortly before midnight, she passed away. I'm returning your letter and photograph with this one.

"Oh no," said Lourdes, looking up with tears in her eyes. "Miss Ellington must have been so sad!" She put the letter on the table.

"Sheila Flaherty was her best friend when they were little," said Oscar. "Miss Ellington still wrote her every week. Sometimes I took the letter to the post office for her, and brought Mrs. Flaherty's answer back." Oscar noticed a picture that'd been folded inside the letter, an old black-and-white photo of a baseball team. He read the words inked onto the bottom of the picture. *The Mt. Etna Mountaineers, 1935.* He said, "Pinky Whitney told me about this team. That twelve-year-old girl played for them, the one I was telling you about. The one who struck out Babe Ruth."

He handed the photo to Lourdes.

She turned it over. "Look," she said. "Their names and ages are on the back. Norman Pliner. Age nineteen. Huggsy Strathmore, twenty-one. Dinky Hanrahan, eighteen."

Oscar realized he recognized the names. They were a few of Miss Ellington's old pen pals, although most of them were gone now.

"Sheila Flaherty, seventeen," continued Lourdes. "Eleanor Ethel Smiley, twelve."

"What?" cried Oscar. "Eleanor Ethel *Smiley?* Let me see that." Oscar looked at the curling photo. There in the front row sat a girl who looked about his age, smiling uncertainly at him in grainy black and white, displaying a gap in her teeth. "Eleanor Ethel Smiley was the name of the girl who struck out Babe Ruth? That explains the initials on Miss Ellington's mitt. Eleanor Ethel Smiley is

Eleanor Ethel Ellington. Before she grew up and got married and changed her last name."

At that moment, Oscar spotted something out of place on the messy kitchen table. As he picked it up, it crumbled between his fingers.

"An old hamburger bun?" said Lourdes quizzically.

"Miss Ellington would never leave stale bread lying around her kitchen to attract ants!" said Oscar. "This proves it."

"Proves what?" asked Lourdes.

"Miss Ellington is the one who took the watch from my bread box!" said Oscar. "I hid it in a hamburger bun. She must've sneaked in after you knocked on my door yesterday and stolen it back before Mr. Llimb and Mr. Skerritt could find it."

"So your friend Miss Ellington is the one who struck out Babe Ruth when she was twelve," said Lourdes thoughtfully. "And she's also the one who took the watch you've been looking for. And now she's gone."

"That about sums it up," sighed Oscar.

"Why would she do all that?"

"I have no idea." Oscar stared at the kitchen table, lost in thought.

"Look!" Lourdes exclaimed. She'd sifted through the

jumble of mail on the table to find a yellowed old envelope "'Oscar Indigo,'" Lourdes read. "It's addressed to you! Open it!"

Oscar grabbed the envelope and tore it open. Inside was a faded pair of admission tickets. "'Mt. Etna Mountaineers versus Boston Braves,'" he read. "'Mt. Etna Diamond, April 11, 1935.'"

"Maybe they're stubs she kept as souvenirs, and she wanted you to have them," said Lourdes.

"They're not just stubs. They're tickets. They've never been used," said Oscar, examining them closely.

"But why would Miss Smiley leave two old tickets in an envelope addressed to you?" said Lourdes.

"Because she wants me to come to a game," said Oscar, "at Mt. Etna Diamond. In 1935. And to bring along a friend."

Once they made it to Mt. Etna Diamond, they stood in the dark, wondering what to do next. Oscar read aloud the historical plaque bolted to the gates. He'd never paid attention to it before. CONSTRUCTED 1934 FOR THE CITIZENS OF MT. ETNA. HOME OF THE MT. ETNA MOUNTAINEERS.

As he spoke, ghostly sounds rustled to life around them. The *ayoooga* of old-fashioned automobile horns. The chatter of invisible people passing. The creak of the iron gates swinging open. Which they actually did, the real ones, right in front of Oscar and Lourdes. An unseen kid sang "Take Me Out to the Ball Game." From inside the park came the cries of a hawker selling popcorn and peanuts.

The ground vibrated beneath their feet. With a sizzle and a buzz, the night around them began to disappear in fits and starts. Soon, their surroundings had disintegrated completely, and Oscar and Lourdes began drifting through utter nothing. Oscar took a deep breath to steady himself.

"Oscar? What's happening?" cried Lourdes fearfully, reaching for his hand.

"We must be journeying through the universe," said Oscar. "After all those other things visited us from their times and places, we're the ones traveling now. I think we'll be OK. I think we'll be there soon."

"But where is there?" wondered Lourdes. "We're in the middle of pitch-black zilch!"

"If we can just find a place to turn in these admission tickets, I think we'll see," replied Oscar.

And even as he spoke, around them, another time began to take form.

The ballpark began to reappear, newer, younger, glossier, until they were on solid ground again in front of it. It looked the way it must've looked in Miss Ellington's glory days.

Oscar saw a man in an usher's uniform outside the gate and knew what to do. He handed over the tickets. The usher tore them in two and gave the stubs to Oscar. "What are you waiting for?" he exclaimed. "Step inside!"

The stadium was almost unrecognizable. Fans wore old-fashioned suits and ties and dresses and hats. Oscar's and Lourdes's shorts and T-shirts were nothing like the clothes of the people around them, but nobody seemed to notice.

Oscar and Lourdes took in the splendor as they found their seats. Section D, seats 4 and 5.

On the field, the Mt. Etna Mountaineers warmed up. The Boston Braves were nowhere to be seen. Oscar saw Sheila and Norman and Huggsy—everyone he recognized from Miss Ellington's photo.

Then he heard a girl's voice cry from the direction of the field. "Heavens to Betsy! You're here!"

"Miss Ellington?" Oscar rushed to the edge of the

field. There was Miss Ellington, looking just like herself, only seventy-three years younger.

"Yes. Except that today I'm E. E. Smiley," she replied, turning around to display the name on the back of her uniform. "And for this occasion, I'm twelve years old again."

"I'm Lourdes," said Lourdes. She held her hand out.

"Pleased to meet you, Lourdes," said Miss Ellington, or to be precise, E. E. Smiley. "I've heard all about you. A girl after my own heart."

Lourdes beamed.

"Why didn't you tell me you struck out Babe Ruth! That's incredible! And only twelve years old!" Oscar couldn't contain himself.

"It's a little complicated, Oscar," responded E. E. Smiley.

"Well, I'm glad I know now. And thanks for the tickets," said Oscar. "Are we really in 1935?"

"Yes," said E. E. Smiley, "and no."

"What do you mean?" asked Oscar. The old-timey hawker was selling popcorn a few rows over.

"This is a do-over," said E. E. Smiley. "A second chance. A little favor the universe is doing me for keeping an eye on the cosmic tomato bush all these years."

"Wait. That bush in your backyard is *the* cosmic

tomato bush?" asked Oscar.

"It's more of a scale model," replied E. E. Smiley. "A virtual version, I guess you could say. So I can help keep track of how things are going on the major branches. After I'm gone, by the way, the job falls to you."

"I see," said Oscar. "All right. I think I'm up to it. By the way, if this is a do-over, what's it a do-over of?"

"Of the game when I struck out Babe Ruth," said E. E. Smiley.

"Why would you want a do-over? To relive the memory?" asked Oscar.

"No, I need to prove something to myself," replied E. E. Smiley. "I need to prove I haven't been living a lie. To show I really did strike out the Bambino all those years ago."

"But you definitely did!" declared Oscar.

"I might have. Or my strikeout might have been as legit as that home run of yours, Oscar."

Oscar was about to protest when Miss Ellington cut him off. "Don't—I know all about your homer, Oscar. *And* the watch! I've seen the pterodactyls around town. My last name is *Smiley*. Hector was my grandfather! And he was here in the audience that day. The day I supposedly struck out the Babe."

"So?" asked Oscar.

"He had his watch with him. He could have stopped time and made sure I struck out the Babe."

"He couldn't have had the watch," said Oscar. "He sent it to the Veeder-Klamm Museum for safekeeping. President Roosevelt told him to." But even as Oscar said this, he remembered the newspaper article the watch was wrapped in. It was about the very game Miss Ellington was worried about. Which meant that—

"He had the watch in his pocket while I pitched," said E. E. Smiley, as if reading Oscar's mind. "He didn't get rid of it until *after* my game."

"What difference does that make?" asked Lourdes.

"It always made me wonder," said E. E. Smiley. "It made me wonder if he brought it to stop time. In case I needed assistance striking out Babe Ruth. He was a wonderful grandfather. Sometimes maybe too wonderful. He would've done anything to help me."

"I know your grandfather didn't help you with this!" declared Oscar. "You did it yourself."

"How can you be sure?" asked E. E. Smiley.

"Because he must've known how risky it would be to use the watch, no matter how much he wanted you to succeed," said Oscar.

"But how could a twelve-year-old strike out Babe Ruth

without help?" asked E. E. Smiley.

"By throwing the perfect pitch!" replied Oscar.

"Well, I never believed I had the stuff to accomplish that," said E. E. Smiley. "Especially after what Babe Ruth said when it was all over."

"What did he say?" asked Lourdes.

"That I was pretty good for a girl," said E. E. Smiley.

"I know the feeling," muttered Lourdes.

"I heard it so much, and not just from him, that I'd started to believe maybe I *was* only pretty good—for a girl. I doubted myself. I always did doubt myself. That's why I still halfway believe I only pitched that strikeout because my grandfather pulled a fast one by halting time with his watch. And because I had doubts, I quit. As soon as the inning was over. I quit baseball and I never played again. Can you believe that?"

"You could've asked your grandfather if he used the watch," said Oscar.

"I didn't want to," said E. E. Smiley.

"Why not?" asked Lourdes.

"Well, like I said. Down deep, I never really believed I got that pitch past Mr. Ruth without help," said Miss Ellington. "And I felt like living in doubt was better than knowing for sure."

"Why did you take the watch from the museum again after so many years?" asked Oscar.

"As I got older, and my friends began leaving me behind, I started to wonder if I'd really lived the life I was meant to. I always wondered if I could've played in the major leagues. Even if I was a girl, and even if they'd never have let me, I wanted to know if I *could've*. Do you know what I mean?"

"I do," Lourdes declared emphatically.

"And if you struck out Babe Ruth, you definitely could've," added Oscar.

"But you see, I *wasn't* sure if I'd struck out Babe Ruth," said Miss Ellington.

"So why take the watch? Was there some way to use it to find out after all that time what had really happened?" asked Oscar.

"No. I took the watch to *smash* it, so I wouldn't be *tempted* to use it to find out," said E. E. Smiley. "Unfortunately, those men came before I could find the crab hammer to do the deed. I didn't know what they wanted, but I knew it couldn't be good. So I gave you the watch to get it out of there. I didn't know you'd use it before I could get it back."

"Well, I did," said Oscar ruefully. "I'm so very sorry."

"No use crying over spilled milk, Oscar. Because here we are. Back where it all began. Settling the question for good," said E. E. Smiley. "Did I really strike out Babe Ruth?"

"Why did you invite Oscar and me?" asked Lourdes.

"To make sure my grandfather doesn't use his watch when I throw Babe Ruth the third strike," said E. E. Smiley. "Your seats are next to his. Watch to be sure he doesn't stop time, and run to the plate, and slip the ball past the Babe, or pull some other kind of trick the way that—"

"I did," supplied Oscar.

"Yes," agreed E. E. Smiley. "The way you did. I know he might be tempted. Did I mention I'm his favorite grandchild? And he always wants me to be happy. His judgment could be clouded. He might try to help me."

"We'll keep an eye out," said Lourdes.

Oscar said, "I'm just excited I get to see you play! And after your last game, you can come to *our* last game. See us win fair and square and fix the universe!"

Miss Ellington looked sad and didn't say anything.

"What is it?" Oscar asked. Her face had changed. "You are coming back, aren't you?" asked Oscar, fearing the answer.

"Oscar," E. E. Smiley sighed. "I'm not returning after

this game. I'm going to stay with my teammates. I'm sorry. I have to keep moving forward. I miss my friends, my old friends. And it's time for me to leave the universe I lived in with you. I know you'll understand."

Oscar nodded. He thought he understood. He thought of the Wildcats, how they'd turned into his friends over the years, supporting each other through it all. He thought of Miss Ellington's letters, her friends steadily slipping away from her. "But I'll miss you," said Oscar. "In our universe."

"You're one of the best friends I ever had," said E. E. Smiley.

"Thanks," said Oscar. "And you're the one of the best friends I've ever had."

"That puts me in good company," replied E. E. Smiley, grinning at Lourdes. "And now. Two last things. Please keep an eye on the tomato bush for me. And please keep your eyes open when you swing."

"I will," said Oscar. "And I do!"

"No, you don't," said E. E. Smiley. "I've been telling you for years."

"Yes, I do," said Oscar.

"What does it look like when you hit the ball?" asked E. E. Smiley.

"I don't know," said Oscar.

"You should. Watch the ball until the bat meets it. Watch it until you see the barrel touch the leather. Watch it until you hear the crack. Watch it, or you won't beat the Yankees. And that's the most important thing in your universe! Good-bye, Oscar Indigo." With that, she ran across the diamond to finish warming up with her team.

By the time the umpire called, "Play ball!" there were five thousand people in the stands. E. E. Smiley stood ready on the mound. The Mt. Etna Mountaineers ranged around the field behind her. Oscar and Lourdes sat patiently watching the action. No sign of E. E. Smiley's grandfather yet, though.

The Boston Braves, recently arrived from many different points in time and space to play in the do-over, watched her curiously from the dugout.

And finally Babe Ruth emerged, swinging his bat casually, looking a little embarrassed at the prospect of facing a twelve-year-old girl. Lourdes loudly cheered E. E. Smiley on. Oscar had never seen Lourdes smile this much before.

E. E. Smiley didn't waste any time pitching to Babe.

She wound up and threw a wicked sinker. "Steeeerike one!" cried the umpire. She sure hadn't needed any help with that one.

Oscar was impressed. Lourdes whooped.

"That pitch is called The Drop," said a man who was settling into the seat beside Oscar and Lourdes. "I happen to know because that's my granddaughter pitching. Eleanor Ethel. I'm very proud of her. By the way, my name is Hector Smiley." He put out his hand to shake.

"I'm Oscar Indigo," said Oscar.

"And I'm Lourdes Mangubat," said Lourdes.

"Nice to meet you both! Popcorn?" Hector leaned over to offer some. As Oscar munched, he observed Hector out of the corner of his eye. No sign of the watch yet. But as E. E. Smiley readied for the next pitch, Oscar watched Hector's fingers inching toward the pocket of his shirt. And Oscar saw the watch's unmistakable outline in the pocket.

On the field, Babe Ruth smiled, cocked his bat, and set his feet.

Hector Smiley reached into his pocket and slid out the watch.

E. E. Smiley wound up and delivered The Drop again.

The Sultan of Swat took a staggering cut at the ball. And missed. Hector Smiley never touched the red button.

Strike two for E. E. Smiley.

The hometown crowd went wild.

Babe Ruth shrugged. And he dimly smiled.

"That's my girl!" said Hector Smiley.

"Fire it in there!" cried Oscar.

"Bring the heat!" cried Lourdes.

E. E. Smiley sized up the plate like a ten-time all-star.

Next to Oscar, Hector Smiley clutched the watch with his finger on the button. For a moment, Oscar felt the temptation to snatch it away before he used it, but he'd learned his lesson about interfering with the workings of the watch, so he kept still.

On the mound, E. E. Smiley wound up and lobbed what looked like an easy floater. The toss danced through the air, wobbling and bouncing and never flying straight. Babe Ruth's eyes zeroed in on it. It was a beautiful, crazy pitch. And Oscar could tell it was destined to fool the Babe.

Hector Smiley's finger tensed over the watch button.

Oscar held his breath. Lourdes, who was also watching Hector Smiley's finger, twitched.

But as the pitch neared the plate, Hector Smiley let his finger relax. He realized Babe had no hope. Hector Smiley's granddaughter was as good as everybody had believed. Because Babe Ruth stood frozen by the deceptiveness of her pitch. And the ball sailed straight over home and into the catcher's mitt.

"Steeeeee-rike three! Yer out!" cried the ump.

Hector Smiley slid the watch into his pocket, unused, and breathed a sigh of relief.

E. E. Smiley had done it all on her own.

Never before had such cheering been heard in Mt. Etna. In all the noise and jubilation, Babe Ruth muttered something to E. E. Smiley, then broke his bat over his knee, threw the pieces on the ground.

E.E. Smiley just shrugged.

"Atta girl!" cried Hector Smiley. "Atta girl!"

From the mound, E. E. Smiley gazed at Oscar. Oscar shot back a thumbs-up. "You did it!" he called. She smiled brilliantly, and waved, and turned to face the next Boston Brave batter.

"Oh, do you know my granddaughter?" asked Hector Smiley.

"She's one of my best friends," replied Oscar.

But Hector Smiley had already begun to fade from beside him. On the mound, E. E. Smiley became thin and ghostly. In a matter of seconds, Oscar and Lourdes found themselves sitting in a deserted ballpark, the night pressing in on them from every direction, in the darkness before dawn.

"She did it," said Oscar. "She really did it!"

Lourdes gave him a high five.

In the seat where Hector Smiley had been sitting lay the watch, ticking away in the starlight.

"Yessssssss," said Oscar quietly, scooping it up. "Now we just have to beat the Yankees, and I have to give nineteen seconds back to the universe."

In the dimness, he turned the watch over and peered at the inscriptions weaving in and out of each other on the back. A new one leaped out at him. Oscar read it in a whisper. "'How did it get so late so soon?'"

"By the way, she's right about your eyes," Lourdes said as they walked home. The suns were rising in the morning sky by now.

"What about them?" asked Oscar.

"You always close them at the last second."

"No I don't," said Oscar.

"Yes you do," said Lourdes.

"No, I don't," said Oscar. "But maybe we can get some batting practice in before the game tonight."

"You never quit, do you?" said Lourdes. "Sure, we'll practice, but first, let's ask my mom to make breakfast for us."

Mangoes

Lourdes's kitchen blazed with sunlight and smelled lush with the aroma of tropical fruit. At the counter, a small woman sliced up mangoes with a knife.

"Mom," said Lourdes, "this is Oscar Indigo. Oscar, this is my mom."

"Hello, Mrs. Mangubat," said Oscar.

"Hi, Oscar! I'm cutting up some mangoes for breakfast," said Mrs. Mangubat. "Don't ask how I got them. It's an international secret!" She winked. "Want one?"

Oscar had never had a mango before. They seemed to come in a little bowl of their own rind. "What do I do?" he asked when she handed him one.

"Spoon it up out of the skin. Aren't they good?"

"This," Oscar exclaimed once he'd tried one, "is the most delicious thing I've ever eaten."

"These aren't even the best. You should go to the Philippines. Try them fresh," said Mrs. Mangubat. "Lourdes and I will take you next time we go, and you'll see! For now, I'm off to work. Bye!" Oscar couldn't help but laugh at how different Lourdes was from her bubbly mother.

"And now," Lourdes said, once they'd finished the mangoes and her mom had pulled out of the driveway, "about your little habit of batting with your eyes closed."

"I said it before, I don't do that!" said Oscar. "My eyes are always open!"

"We'll see about that," said Lourdes. "Come on." She tucked a bat under her arm, grabbed a glove and ball, and opened the back door for Oscar.

Lourdes pulled an old soccer net behind Oscar like a backstop. Then she walked far enough away so that it seemed like she was on the mound and turned to throw him a slow, easy pitch. Oscar swung. And missed. The ball hit the net behind him.

"See! You blinked," cried Lourdes.

"I didn't!" protested Oscar.

"What did the ball look like when it went by?" asked Lourdes.

"I don't know. Like a baseball," said Oscar.

"Which way was it spinning?" asked Lourdes.

"What? How am I supposed to know that?" said Oscar.

"By keeping your eyes open," said Lourdes. "Tell me, honestly, what happens when you're at bat, Oscar?"

"I get scared," said Oscar. "I'm afraid I'll miss. I hear a roar in my ears and everything gets blurry. And I whiff. Every stinking time."

"Then don't get scared," said Lourdes.

"Easy for you to say," said Oscar.

"Take three deep breaths," said Lourdes. "Imagine how awesome it's going to feel when you get a hit. And then watch the ball until your bat hits it, just like E. E. Smiley said." She reached into her pocket and came over to Oscar. "Also, let's prop your eyes open with these tooth-picks." She snapped one in half and reached for Oscar's left eye.

"Wait," protested Oscar. "You're making a joke, right? The great no-nonsense Lourdes Mangubat is kidding around?"

"You never know with me," answered Lourdes. But she was smiling, and Oscar knew she was teasing. "Just don't close your eyes. I'll keep the toothpicks in my pocket in case."

Lourdes walked back to her spot. "Now. Let's try again." Oscar took three breaths and thought about how awesome it would be to hit her next pitch. And not to have his eyelids propped open with toothpicks. Just in case Lourdes *wasn't* joking. Lourdes let her pitch go. Oscar waited. And watched. And swung. And saw his bat hit the ball. And watched the ball fly over Lourdes's head into the trees behind her yard. It lodged in a tall one with tentacles.

"Wow!" Oscar cried.

"That's better," said Lourdes after she wrested the ball away from the tree. "And now, if you can get Taser to throw you a fastball like that, you might even be able to blast a home run."

"How?" asked Oscar. "When I hit it the other night, after I stopped time, while it was dangling in the air, the ball barely made it to the edge of the infield."

"That's because the ball wasn't moving when you hit it," said Lourdes. "Watch carefully, and hit this."

She wound up and threw a smoking fastball. Oscar watched closely and met the ball with his bat. *Blam!* It ricocheted off like a meteor. It flew over the trees and disappeared.

"How did I do that?" asked Oscar wonderingly.

"*You* didn't. We *both* did. The momentum of my pitch plus the force of your swing added up to a shot over the trees. If you can get Taser to throw you a fastball tomorrow, then boom, Taser's hummer will bounce right off your bat and take the ball over his head, over the wall, out of the park."

"How do I get Taser to throw the ball that hard?" asked Oscar. "How do we even know Taser will be pitching? He's not supposed to. He's been on the mound the past two games in a row."

"His mom will figure out something. She always does," replied Lourdes. "So you have to get the better of him. You need to make him mad. Act like you think you can hit his pitch. Act like you think you're as good as he is. It makes him furious. And when he gets angry, he gets careless, and he throws a fastball over the middle of the plate. You've seen him do it."

"I sure have," said Oscar. "I guess I can act like I think I'm as good as he is. Because I am as good as he is."

"Darn right," said Lourdes.

And so Oscar Indigo, after the best batting practice of his life, figured out how to beat the Yankees.

All he had to do now was figure out how to put the

nineteen seconds back.

In the meantime, he thought it would be a good idea to fix as many of the things he'd wrecked as possible. Starting with his mother's job.

Mr. Rossini

Oscar left Lourdes's house and decided to make a quick detour on his way home. To Rossini's. It was still morning, so the restaurant wasn't open, but Oscar could see Mr. Rossini, old, gray, and as round as a croquet ball, inside at a table by the window, sliding white napkins into gold rings.

Oscar tapped on the window.

Mr. Rossini waved him inside.

"Mr. Rossini," said Oscar. "You should come to the big game tonight."

"Football?" he asked hopefully in his thick Italian accent.

"No," said Oscar. "Baseball."

"Foo," said Mr. Rossini. "In Italy, we laugh at that. And then fall asleep. What a slow sport!"

"But you might like it," persisted Oscar.

"I might," allowed Mr. Rossini. "Though I never done before." After a pause, he said, "Hey, Oscar. I miss seeing you and your mama around here. I especially miss your mama's singing!"

"I wanted to talk to you about that," said Oscar. He pulled his phone out of his pocket. "I have something for you to listen to." After leaving Lourdes's house, Oscar had racked his brains trying to figure out how to get those nineteen seconds back. Perhaps, he thought, if he undid all the damage they had done, he could fix things. He didn't know how to fix that second sun, but he could start small: by getting his mom a job to make up for the one she'd lost.

Oscar played the recording he'd made of her sorrowful singing from the night before. The sad refrains filled up the quiet restaurant.

"That is quite beautiful," said Mr. Rossini.

Oscar smiled and left Mr. Rossini lost in a reflective daze.

Oscar was on a roll. Oscar was going to fix the universe.

Game Three of the Series

There were so many TV trucks crowded around Mt. Etna Diamond that Oscar's mom had to park six blocks away. Three news helicopters hovered overhead, and the *whap whap whap* of their rotors made Oscar feel like he was about to play baseball in a combat zone. Even higher overhead, three hundred feet above the choppers, the Goodyear Blimp circled.

While Oscar stared upward in wonder at all the aircraft, Taser Tompkins shouldered him to the dirt. Robocop snickered. "Nice going, genius," said Taser. "The story of the underdog Wildcats and their little home-run hero is going viral. Now the whole country will be watching when the Yankees smash you guys like electric guitars." They turned and stamped away toward their dugout, but not before Robocop kicked dirt on Oscar's uniform pants.

Slowly, Oscar climbed to his feet.

"Oscar, have you got a second?" cried a woman's voice over the roar of the helicopters.

Oscar squinted through the dust to see Vern and Suzy, earpieces in place, hair flying, as they raced toward him with their microphones. This time, they weren't just figments of his imagination. They were really at the game.

"Tell us your secret, Oscar Indigo," requested Vern.

"How have the Wildcats made it this far?" prodded Suzy. "The whole country wants to know."

"A lot of dedication," replied Oscar. "And a little luck."

"And gallons of OscarAde!" shouted Bobby Farouk, bombing the interview.

"And what is OscarAde?" asked Suzy as security guards politely but firmly removed Bobby from the picture.

"Our team's favorite sports drink," replied Bobby, popping back in. "It contains a secret ingredient."

"What's the secret ingredient? Your fans will want to know," said Vern.

"Ask Oscar," said Bobby. "He makes it. Gotta go." This time, the security guards meant business.

"Oscar?" prompted Vern, pointing the mike at him.

"If I told you, it wouldn't be secret, would it?" replied Oscar cagily.

"I guess not," said Vern, scratching his head in disappointment.

Once he and Suzy finished the interview, they made their way toward the broadcast desk. Butterflies took flight in Oscar's stomach. The Wildcats *had* to win this. But even with high spirits and practice—could they really beat the Yankees? And for that matter, could he find a way to put those nineteen seconds back where they belonged? Wherever that might be? Evidence that the universe was crumbling rapidly lay all around. The double suns burned in the sky. His mom was yelling in the stands—until Mr. Rossini went up to her and began a quiet conversation . . . well, maybe that was a good sign. Still, Oscar had his work cut out for him.

Mr. Llimb and Mr. Skerritt met him at the dugout gate. "Any luck?" they asked.

"Some." Oscar showed them the watch he'd been holding on to since he'd retrieved it from Hector Smiley's seat at the do-over baseball game. "Managed to get this back, which is a starting point, I guess."

"Good!" Mr. Llimb exclaimed. "Why don't you hold

on to that until T. Buffington Smiley arrives . . . as long as you're not tempted to—"

"I've learned my lesson." Oscar blushed. "I'm not pushing the button ever again. Is T. Buffington Smiley coming?"

"Yes, he has some important information for you and your team," Mr. Skerritt said. "He should be here soon. He had one last wave to ride before he left the beach."

"Hopefully he can tell me how to get those nineteen seconds back. I'm starting to get worried!" fretted Oscar.

Sounds of the team getting ready called his attention back to the field.

"Anyway, before you go join your pals, we bought something for you," said Mr. Llimb self-consciously. "See, Mr. Skerritt and I picked out a new pair of baseball shoes. We didn't know what style you'd like. So we just guessed." He shyly brought a shoe box from behind his back and revealed a pair of glistening, black, handmade spikes, highlighted by five red stripes apiece.

"Just a little something you probably wouldn't have bought for yourself," threw in Mr. Skerritt.

"They're spectacular!" said Oscar. "I love them!"

"Knock 'em dead, ace," said Mr. Llimb.

* * *

"I guess I better make a speech," said Coach Ron as the team collected up in the dugout. "Ahem. Dearly beloved, we are gathered here today—"

"Coach," interrupted Oscar, "I've got this."

"I have this whole thing about General Custer," Coach Ron said, gesturing distractedly at his notes. "And how he stood up to adversity. I think it'll get us through all our problems."

"It won't, Coach, because I'm the problem," said Oscar. The team was silent. "The problem with our team, and with everything else. I'm the reason the whole universe has gone nuts."

"No way," said Steve Brinkley.

"Way," said Oscar. "Because I cheated. I didn't hit that home run. I used a device that stops time to make it look like I'd hit a home run. But there were some significant repercussions—namely, I broke the universe and now we're in trouble."

"Wait a minute," said Axel Machado. "Are you the reason there are two suns and no bees and tsunamis every day on the shore?"

"Well," said Oscar, "yes."

"I don't believe it," said Axel. "You're such a nice guy."

"Tell them, Lourdes," said Oscar. "It's important for the team to know."

"He did it," confirmed Lourdes. "It's hard to believe, but he did. I know for a fact."

"This changes everything," said Kevin. "I mean, we don't even deserve to be tied 1–1 with the Yankees. I'm sorry, Oscar, but we might as well give up! We're losers. We'll always be losers even with Lourdes and OscarAde. Go tell Suzy and Vern so they can break the story, and let's go home."

The team sat quietly. No one could really deny what Kevin had said. News helicopters hummed in the silence. Oscar didn't know what to say. He only wished T. Buffington Smiley were there to give him advice. And just like that, footsteps sounded outside.

"Hello?" T. Buffington Smiley stepped into the dugout, saying, "Sorry I'm late! You haven't given up, yet, right? I have last-minute information that might help."

"Who is this guy?" asked Coach Ron.

"Let me introduce Professor T. Buffington Smiley," said Oscar. "He's a famous scientist."

"Hi, all! Sorry I'm late. Pterodactyls. What I came to say is that, firstly, you actually *do* deserve to be tied with the Yankees," said T. Buffington Smiley. "See, I did a little computation. It wasn't even that hard. You cheated to win game one, we all know that." Oscar could feel himself blushing. "But they cheated to win game two!" Professor Smiley finished triumphantly.

"Right! They lied so Taser could pitch! I knew it! Remember, kids?" Coach Ron was beside himself.

"Which puts you even at 1–1," said T. Buffington Smiley. "And now, here is what I came to say: You need to win."

"Of course we do!" said Kevin.

"No, the fate of the universe depends on it. Oscar might not have told you the whole story, because he doesn't want to worry you, but I will. To fix this thing, you need to achieve victory. If you guys don't beat the Yankees fair and square and Oscar doesn't figure out how to put back the nineteen seconds he took, our universe will go downhill with lightning speed. Taser Tompkins and Robocop Roberts and the rest of the Yankees and everyone like them will always win, every game they play. And that's just for starters, because in addition, there will be hordes of invading pterodactyls and sinister trees waving tentacles, and unhappy parents will never leave their dead-end jobs, and absent fathers will miss important games, and the second sun will slowly cook earth until nothing can live on it, and then our universe will break off the cosmic plant that sustains it, and we'll all—"

"We get the picture, Professor Smiley," said Oscar.

"There's one more thing," said the professor. "Oscar, by watching the waves and interpreting their motions, I have been able to deduce that *you need to replace what you took when time was stopped.* You, Oscar, need to hit your own home run."

"OK, Professor," said Oscar. "I'm on it."

"Now. Go out there and win!" said T. Buffington Smiley.

"We're the Wildcats! We're the best! We will!" cried Oscar. And with that, he launched into the team cheer as all the Wildcats joined in:

"East Mt. Etna, East Mt. Etna, East Mt. Etna, wow! Ain't nobody gonna keep the Wildcats down!"

Oscar at the Bat

"The top of the first!" exclaimed Coach Ron, spreading his arms expansively. Either Coach Ron had already forgotten what exactly they stood to lose if this game went wrong, or he was putting on a brave face for the benefit of his players. Which seemed a lot more likely. "The game stretching out before us in all its glory. Like the ocean greeting a sailor. Like the moon welcoming Neil Armstrong. Like Kansas beckoning farmers. Like the shores of Ellis Island promising my great-grandfather Teodascz that the future will be bright."

"Right, Coach," said Axel as he watched Lourdes take her warm-up tosses on the mound. "The top of the first is exactly like that . . . except it will all slowly cease to exist anymore if we don't win today."

Coach Ron harrumphed. "We're gonna win," he said.

The ump called, "Batter up!"

The first Yankee headed to the plate. Taser Tompkins.

Oscar glanced at Coach Ron, who said, "I already talked to the umpire. Last game's lineup card was destroyed in a mysterious laundry accident. The ump feels terrible. But since there's no solid proof Taser pitched that game, he's pitching again."

"Lourdes and I sort of figured this would happen," said Oscar. "We even planned on it." He glanced at Lourdes on the mound. He could tell she was rattled by the stakes. She fidgeted on the pitching rubber, and a voice called, "Mow them down, Lourdes Mangubat!" It was her mother.

"You own this guy, Lourdes!" cried Oscar's mom, rattling the aluminum bats in their rack with her opera-singer voice. Oscar noticed his dad was nowhere to be seen, but, he realized, he wasn't surprised. And anyway, there were Mr. Llimb and Mr. Skerritt, off toward right, and behind home plate, T. Buffington Smiley and Mrs. Mangubat. He couldn't help but think how much things had changed since he'd accidentally busted Lourdes's toe and started this whole thing. They hadn't even been friends then, and now they were going to fix the universe together.

"You got this, Lourdes!" Oscar chimed in.

At the plate, Taser glanced nervously at the sky, where two suns were blazing. Then Taser turned his glare at Lourdes, who was set on the mound.

"Come on, Taser! She's only a girl! Don't look so scared!" Taser's mom hollered from the stands.

Oscar saw a confident glimmer in Lourdes's eyes, instead of her usual distant stare. No doubt Lourdes was thinking about E. E. Smiley and the way she'd beat Babe Ruth. She wound up and delivered her first pitch. Oscar couldn't believe his eyes. The ball flew straight down the middle and then plummeted toward Taser's feet. The Drop! Lourdes had picked it up by watching Eleanor Ethel Smiley!

"Steerike one!" cried the umpire.

Taser looked out at the mound and snarled. But it was no use. Lourdes delivered two more pitches like the first and struck him out. And for good measure, she struck out the next two batters, Bif Stroganoff and Robocop.

Lourdes came in from the field, grabbed her bat, and headed out to lead off the bottom of the inning. Taser awaited her on the mound.

Taser stared at Lourdes for ten solid seconds, as if to ice her. Then he wound up and pitched. Lourdes smashed his toss straight toward the left-field fence.

As the ball flew over his head, Taser flung his glove to the ground in disgust. This ball was clearly headed out of the park. But before Lourdes even made it to first, a wind began to blow, pushing Lourdes's hit into foul territory.

"Wave it back in, Lourdes!" cried Oscar. "Just like Carlton Fisk!" Lourdes waved, but the universe was different now than it had been in Carlton's day, and the ball kept drifting foul, until it dropped into a thicket of blackberry bramble that writhed ever so quietly at the far end of the third-base bleachers.

Strike one.

Taser picked up his glove, pounded his fist into it triumphantly like this outcome was what he'd been planning on all along, and waited impatiently for the ump to throw him a new ball.

The wind died down.

Taser threw another pitch. This one, Lourdes hit, but not nearly as well. It dropped into the outfield for a single.

But Taser struck out the next three batters in a row, including Oscar.

So much for the first inning.

"That's OK, guys!" shouted Oscar as the team

prepared to take the field. "We've got eight more innings to score! Let's play defense."

But there actually wasn't much defense to play. Lourdes took the mound and zeroed in on the strike zone, and she mowed down Yankees as if their butts were grass and she were the lawnmower.

Until the top of the sixth, when Taser got on base with a single and stole second. Dusty committed an error, and Taser scored. Yankees 1, Wildcats 0.

And then, in the top of the seventh, Lourdes gave up a double and a single, allowing one more run before she managed to retire the side. Yankees 2, Wildcats 0. Oscar expected to see her as upset as she'd been when she gave up runs to the opposition in the game before. But Lourdes looked calm and determined. Not at all flustered by what had happened. "Let's go get 'em, Wildcats!" she shouted as she came back to the dugout.

Her enthusiasm inspired hope in Oscar. "It's OK, team!" cried Oscar. "We've got these guys right where we want them!" He was passing out OscarAde, doing jumping jacks, taking practice swings to stay upbeat. The looks of despair on his teammates' faces were getting to him, though.

But slowly, the enthusiasm shown by Oscar and

Lourdes seemed to take hold of the Wildcats. In the top of the eighth, Steve Brinkley hit an infield single to make it to first. And Taser made a mistake. He ignored his coach's orders to walk Lourdes. He threw her two curveballs, which she missed by a mile.

And since the first two curveballs had worked so well, he threw one more. And Lourdes was waiting. She put the hurt on it. Her shot cleared the centerfield fence by twenty feet.

Oscar felt his spirits lift. Maybe they could do it— they could actually save the universe. They could beat the Yankees.

But after Steve and Lourdes had rounded the bases, Taser got himself together. He struck out Axel Machado like Axel was wearing a blindfold.

End of the inning. The teams were tied 2–2.

Taser stomped into the dugout, threw his glove at the wall, and came right back out and hit a homer off Lourdes. But after that, Lourdes held it together and got out of the top of the ninth with no more damage. Yankees 3, Wildcats 2.

"This is more runs than I've given up in my whole life," Lourdes told the team. Yet her voice was light, almost cheerful.

"It's all gonna be OK," said Coach Ron. "We're still in the game. It's the bottom of the ninth inning, but we've got this. One chance is all we need!"

"Right!" Lourdes said. "And we've kept each other going so far. I know we'll get the victory. It doesn't matter how, it just matters that we do!" She smiled and gave Carlissimo Fong a high five. "So we still have a chance. Right, Oscar?"

"Exactly right," replied Oscar. He tried not to look as nervous as he felt.

From their perch at the top of the stands, Suzy and Vern could be heard broadcasting the action.

The series is tied, Vern.

And the Yankees lead in this, the final game, Suzy.

It's winner take all, Vern. The Wildcats better put it in gear.

Now that they were actually at the game, truly broadcasting, in their actual voices, Oscar could tell that down deep, despite their attempts to sound neutral, Suzy and Vern really wanted the Wildcats to win. Oscar took that as a good sign.

Oscar handed Lourdes her bat as she headed out to start the bottom of the ninth. "I'll pass on the OscarAde," she said. "Just to be safe." She smiled and Oscar smiled back.

"No matter how this turns out," said Oscar, "I'll always be glad we made friends."

"We're great teammates, aren't we?" asked Lourdes.

"The best," said Oscar.

"Just keep your eyes open when you come up to bat. Remember my backyard. Think about the toothpicks," said Lourdes.

"You're joking about those. I know it," said Oscar. "But I'll remember. I'll keep my eyes open. Good luck out there, Lourdes."

"Thanks, Oscar," said Lourdes. She took the long walk to the plate to lead off the bottom of the ninth.

And right away, Lourdes whacked a leadoff single on a wobbly fastball from Taser.

But Taser set down the next two batters, Kamran and Axel. Two outs. One more, and the game was over—no joy, no championship, no future, no universe. A dead silence descended on the diamond.

So came Oscar's turn to bat. He downed a half-pint of OscarAde, grimaced, made sure his new shoes were on tight, and made his way to the plate. This was it. The

Wildcats were behind. They were depending on Oscar to get them out of this. And it wasn't just the Wildcats. There was also Oscar's mom, T. Buffington Smiley, Lourdes and her mom, Mr. Llimb and Mr. Skerritt—everyone was depending on him. He'd never hit a homer before—how was he supposed to hit one now?

Taser Tompkins toed the rubber. He eyeballed Oscar. He stepped off the mound. He looked almost casual, like this didn't matter. Like the game already belonged to the Yankees. He didn't know that if he won, the whole universe would lose.

But that's how it had to be. Oscar couldn't exactly walk out to the mound and say, "Please take it easy on me." Because the Wildcats had to win fair and square, and that wouldn't happen if Taser lost the game on purpose, now, would it?

Taser stepped back onto the mound. He watched his catcher, Bif Stroganoff, for the proper signal.

In the meantime, Taser's lovely mom shouted, "That girl is stealing second base!"

Taser spun and threw. But it was too late. Lourdes was too fast for him. She was too fast for any of them. She cruised into second standing up.

Taser chuckled like he didn't care. Like it didn't

matter. Like the Yankees were going to win anyway, this game, every game, all the time, forever, the way it had always been, the way it would always be, until the end of the universe.

"It's OK, Oscar," shouted Oscar's mom. "You can do it. I'm sure."

"One thousand percent definitely! No doubt!" added T. Buffington Smiley.

Which was about nine hundred percent *too* sure to sound convincing. Oscar knew that T. Buffington Smiley would never make a mathematical miscalculation like this unless he were really, really, nervous.

Oscar stepped to the plate.

The sky bloomed with color from the two suns. This was Oscar's last chance to hit the homer. His last chance to save the universe.

Taser stared at Lourdes on second, daring her to try to steal third. Lourdes's eyes went wide in the glare of his stare, and she dropped her gaze timidly to the dirt, edging safely back toward second. Taser sneered at her display of faintheartedness and went into his motion. He delivered.

Oscar chanted to himself *keep your eyes open keep your eyes open*, but as soon as the pitch was delivered, a roaring began in his ears. He felt the pressure of all the eyes in the stands watching, waiting for him to hit—or strike out. The pitch closed in, the ballpark lights glinted in his eyes, that wicked breeze began to blow, and all of it created one chaotic vortex so bewildering that Oscar couldn't help it. He closed his eyes. And swung. *Whifffff.* Strike one.

"Yeahhhhhhhhh!" rose the cheer from the Yankees bleachers.

"It's OK, Oscar!" his mom yelled.

"Eyes open!" Lourdes called from second base.

Oscar nodded and got back in the box. He had two more shots at this. He could do it.

Taser peered at the pitches Bif was signaling for. He shook his head three times and nodded at the fourth. He smirked like he was thinking about the humiliation and suffering it was about to cause Oscar. He made his move toward home, and as the pitch left his fingertips, Lourdes took off to steal third.

Oscar forced his eyes open and watched the pitch like a hawk. Like a pterodactyl, even. He stood straight and squared his feet, and kept his balance and relaxed and stayed in control of his body and his mind as the ball neared him, and then—nothing. The pressure and panic and the responsibility of saving the universe overwhelmed him and he shut his eyes again. He swung. He missed, of course. Strike two.

But out on the base path, Lourdes had already started her attempt to steal. She flew toward third. Bif Stroganoff leaped up to throw her out, too late. Lourdes slid in head-first, safe by at least six inches.

Finally, for once in his life, Taser Tompkins had the decency to look rattled. Because, as great players from Jackie Robinson to Melvin Upton have shown, it *is* possible to steal home. And if Lourdes did that, she'd tie the game. And then it wouldn't be such a sure bet that the Yankees would win. Not at all.

Taser glared at the plate. His mother's voice was shrill in the nervous quiet: "Don't you let them score!"

Oscar dug his heels in. Another voice rose in the night. "It's not whether you win or lose, Oscar," his mother called. "It's how you play the game."

"Oh, like you would know" came the reply from Mrs. Tompkins. "Loser."

"What a baseball game this is turning out to be, Suzy. Slugger League Championship Series, Yankees 3, Wildcats 2, bottom of the ninth, two outs, no balls, two strikes, tying run on third, winning run at the plate," narrated Vern into his microphone.

"Game of a lifetime. Game of a lifetime. Lourdes Mangubat takes her lead off third, daring Taser Tompkins to throw her out. Tompkins goes into his windup. And Oscar Indigo digs in," said Suzy.

"Lourdes has an excellent jump."

"Taser delivers. Lourdes fakes the steal and scampers back to third, Vern."

"And Oscar Indigo watches Taser's pitch all the way, Suzy. It hums in for a ball."

"Doesn't lift his bat off his shoulder, Vern."

Oscar nodded. He knew it was a ball. This time he'd been able to keep his eyes open long enough to see. By the time he slammed them shut, the pitch had rushed by him well outside the strike zone.

And then Oscar remembered something Lourdes had said. *Make Taser mad. Act like you think you can hit his pitch. Act like you think you're as good as he is. And when he gets angry, he gets careless, and he throws a fastball over the middle of the plate.* Oscar knew just the way to do it.

He squared up and acted like he planned to hit a home run. Like he was Taser's equal. Like he wasn't the least bit scared. He pointed his bat at the outfield fence like Babe Ruth picking his spot, and squared away to hit.

"You got this, Oscar!" Lourdes cheered.

Taser was so furious he had started to shake. And to make matters worse, as he prepared to deliver, Lourdes took off from third.

"She's going! She's attempting a straight steal of home!" cried Suzy.

"She's off to the races!" shouted Vern.

"The pitcher makes his throw toward the plate."

"Lourdes Mangubat just might beat it. But she's stumbled! She's fallen! She struggles to her feet. Oh, this is terrible, Suzy! She's a dead duck."

"She'll be out by a mile, Vern. She has no chance."

But she did have a chance. Oscar knew she had a chance. *He* was her chance. Because he'd gotten the pitch he wanted. While everyone was distracted by Lourdes's antics in the third baseline, Taser had lost control. He'd thrown a perfect fastball dead in the center of the strike zone. Time seemed to slow down. Oscar could count the seams on the ball. He could read the trademark on the leather. He felt his eyes open wide.

Then confusion began to swirl. The ground beneath his feet seemed to disintegrate, but now, it wasn't like a black hole sucking everything in. It was like the Big Bang, exploding with a force unimaginable by the ordinary human mind. But this wasn't like the previous times when he'd shut his eyes in panic. This was different.

"You cannot blow this," Oscar whispered to himself. "This is your last chance. And Dr. Soul's and your mom's and Lourdes's and even Miss Ellington's." If he missed, his mom would move from job to job and from café to café until finally there would be no more cafés, because the universe would end.

The bees would disappear forever. Two suns would bake the earth.

And Taser and Robocop and the rest of the Yankees would win until there were no more games left to win.

And for the remainder of history, Sheila Tompkins would think she was right about everything.

Focusing with all his might, Oscar snapped his bat around to meet the incoming fastball. He kept his gaze locked onto the pitch, fighting to uphold his promise to himself and to Miss Ellington and to Lourdes and to the rest of the universe. And he saw it. He saw the moment his bat met the smoking ball. The *crack* rang out across the diamond. And Oscar Indigo saw Taser Tompkins's wickedest pitch turn into something else: Oscar Indigo's first honest-to-goodness, bona fide homer flying into the night sky. He'd done it. He'd done it! Oscar savored the cheers from the bleachers.

"Groovy, man!" cried T. Buffington Smiley.

"WAHOOO!" cheered his mom.

"Indigo took quite a cut at the ball, Vern!"

"Chin down. Knees bent. Elbows high. Beautiful swing, Suzy."

"And Vern, he had his eyes open!"

"He saved the base runner, Suzy."

"And seems to have knocked the ball over the fence in the process, Vern."

Oscar noticed that Lourdes had climbed to her feet in the base path, and she stood staring at the ball as it flew higher and higher into the weirdly orange twilit sky.

And then the ball began to drop, much too soon, too far away from the fence. What could have been a homer was turning into a dud before his eyes.

"Did he get enough of the pitch, Suzy?"

"Looks like the wind is blowing the ball back into play, Vern."

"The Yankees' outfielder is running to the track, Suzy. I think he's going to make it. Will the ball clear the fence? Or will it drop into his glove?"

Lourdes and Oscar stood transfixed, watching, like everyone else in the park. "It's going—going—going—" Lourdes shouted.

"Get out of here!" screamed Oscar's mom.

"Fly, you stinking baseball!" bellowed Mr. Llimb.

"Or else!" added Mr. Skerritt.

And then the ball halted in flight. Directly above the centerfield fence, so it was impossible to tell whether it would sail over or drop into the glove of the Yankee outfielder standing beneath it.

Nothing moved. No birds flew, no tree branches swayed in any breeze, and celestial objects halted in their orbits. Nobody stirred. Not even Oscar.

He stood frozen, by apprehension, dread, fear. It felt like the end of the universe.

He did his best to move. But he couldn't. And then he felt it. The watch. In his pocket where he'd left it for safekeeping until he had a chance to return it to T. Buffington Smiley. There it was. Ticking.

One second passed. It took all his strength, but Oscar managed to pull the watch out of his pocket.

Another second passed by. The ballpark faded around him.

He found himself floating in nothingness again, just like when he'd traveled to E. E. Smiley's do-over game with Lourdes.

The seconds ticked by. The ones he'd stolen. But they

ticked by without Oscar. He stood frozen. Panic rose in his throat, as if he were paying the universe back with his own fear.

And then, slowly, the baseball diamond reappeared. Bases, infield grass, a pitcher's mound. But it wasn't Oscar's field or his game. He floated gently above the 1935 game. The Mt. Etna Mountaineers were still playing the Braves; time must have slowed down for them, too. Still, they were almost at the end of their exhibition contest. Slowly, Oscar floated into the air above the infield, where he could see everything.

E. E. Smiley stood at the plate. Full count. The bases were loaded. Her team, according to the scoreboard, was down 4–1. The Boston Braves pitcher wound up. He delivered.

The pitch streaked toward the plate. E. E. Smiley, Eleanor Ethel Ellington's younger self, swung for all she was worth. Oscar heard the crack of her bat. The ball rose through the air. It cleared the fence.

The crowd went wild. Her teammates, all young and talented, just like they'd been in the picture on her table, rushed to congratulate her. She'd done it. She'd really done it. She'd stayed in the game and she'd won it. And now she knew. She was good, really good.

Her smile of relief told Oscar she'd found peace. Now she could move on.

E. E. Smiley glanced up and winked at Oscar as he floated in the air above her. Oscar winked back.

And Oscar knew, just like that, he'd done it, too. Stayed in the game, won it fair and square. He and Miss Ellington had proved to themselves and everyone they could do it, and they had.

And slowly, everything around Oscar began to fade and Oscar began to unfreeze. And then, from the dim stillness, his world reappeared around him. As if nothing had ever happened, Oscar once more found himself at the plate in his own game. His whole journey had taken only—nineteen seconds. He had done it. The universe had its nineteen seconds back. Miss Ellington had hit her homer, and now Oscar and the whole stadium held its breath to see if his hit would clear the fence.

In left field, it kept dropping and dropping and . . . it cleared the ivy-choked fence! He'd given the universe its homer back.

The vines immediately quit writhing and shrank back into a nice green crown along the top.

Oscar threw his arms above his head. He jumped two feet in the air. The crowd went wild.

Taser stood staring at the spot where the ball had disappeared, his hands on his hips.

Then he turned, faced Oscar, and shot him a thumbs-up. Because, come on. Anybody would have to admit: that was a righteous shot.

"You did it!" cried Lourdes, dusting off her knees and standing at home.

Oscar would tell Lourdes about E. E. Smiley's triumph later. She would get a kick out of it. But for now, he savored the sound of his friends and family cheering. The world was coming to life again. The strange orange evening light from the double suns that had glared night after night had become the fragile blue of dusk. The second sun had gone. No more tentacles or pterodactyls, either. Mr. Llimb and Mr. Skerritt and T. Buffington Smiley whooped from the bleachers. His mom's cheers filled the air with sweet music. He'd done it.

And as he took off for first, nobody noticed Oscar Indigo reach into the pocket of his uniform.

As he rounded second, nobody saw him pull his hand back out.

As he touched third, nobody glimpsed the golden gleam in his fist.

As he sprinted home and jumped into the waiting

arms of Lourdes Mangubat, Bobby Farouk, Axel Machado, Kevin Truax, Carlissimo Fong, Steve Brinkley, and the rest, nobody spied a large, old-fashioned railroad watch fall to the dirt, only to be ground to bits beneath the crush of the Marlborough County Champion East Mt. Etna Wildcats, who were busy dogpiling the stuffing out of their hero, Oscar Indigo.

Rossini's

The next evening, the light of the sun poured through the plate glass window of Rossini's. Just the sun, the regular sun, the one and only sun. Scientists reported that the rogue star had somehow managed to escape through a nineteen-second gap in the gravitational field of the solar system the night before, right around the time Oscar had hit his historic home run, and it had disappeared into space.

In the red leather booth in the corner, the best table in the place, sat Lourdes and Oscar and their two mothers. "Spaghetti marinara for the champions—and my next star employee, Ms. Indigo. On the house," said Mr. Rossini, setting down the plates himself. "And a bottle of bubbly water. Compliments of the gentlemen at the corner table."

Mr. Llimb and Mr. Skerritt, suits beautifully cleaned and pressed, raised their glasses in salute.

Oscar lifted his in return. "I would like to propose a toast," he proclaimed, holding his glass up in the light. "To the best baseball player in Pennsylvania."

"To the best teammate in the world," added Lourdes.

"To Lourdes," said Lourdes's mom.

"To Oscar," said Oscar's mom.

"To good times," said Mr. Llimb.

"To friendship," said Mr. Skerritt.

"Cheers!" said Oscar.

And they clinked glasses and enjoyed the evening, and there was not a pterodactyl in sight.

Acknowledgments

This book owes its existence to Alice Jerman and Jennifer Carlson, who cheered for every swing and every miss and did their fair share of coaching along the way. Thanks to Jennifer Klonsky for the care and feeding of the author. Thanks to Marisa de los Santos for innumerable game-time strategy sessions.

Thanks to the 1975 Boston Red Sox, the 2004 Boston Red Sox, the 2008 Philadelphia Phillies, the 2016 Chicago Cubs, and the entire 1973 Conway, Arkansas, Buddy League.

Thanks to Professor George Thompson and the Thompson boys for many thrilling seasons of backyard baseball.

Thanks to Andy Smith, Sarah Creech, Alison Klapthor, Michelle Cunningham, Mitchell Thorpe, Meaghan

Finnerty, Renée Cafiero, and the entire HarperCollins Children's team!

And thanks to my dad for showing me how to oil a glove.

YOU MAY ALSO LIKE

"Wry, bizarre, and as audacious as Henry himself, this is one fantasy/adventure not to be missed."
—*School Library Journal*

HARPER
An Imprint of HarperCollinsPublishers

www.harpercollinschildrens.com